UP, PUP AND AWAY

SPELLBOUND HOUND MAGIC AND MYSTERY BOOK 7

JEANNIE WYCHERLEY

Up, Pup and Away

Spellbound Hound Magic and Mystery Book 7

BY

JEANNIE WYCHERLEY

Bark at the Moon Books

Sign up for Jeannie's newsletter:

www.subscribepage.com/JeannieWycherleyWonky

Up, Pup and Away was edited by Christine L Baker

Cover design by Cover Affairs.
Formatting by Tammy
Proofreading by Johnny Bon Bon

Please note: This book is set in England in the United Kingdom.
It uses British English spellings and idioms.

CHAPTER ONE

Toby was minding his own business.

On this occasion, minding his own business meant drawing. He had his pot of coloured pens to hand—or paw, if you prefer—and was putting the finishing touches to his work. He was more Picasso than Rembrandt, more Munch than Rubens, but there's nothing wrong with that, is there?

The rain hammered down on the shack roof, but Toby barely heard it. He cocked his head and examined his picture. The eyes weren't quite right. It was difficult to get the glow he was after because he didn't have a silver felt tip. The grey didn't quite capture the supernatural quality—the sheer unearthliness—of the woman's gaze.

"Quite the masterpiece that, innit?" Salvatore

Messio, also known as Sal, the rat Toby had recently befriended while trying to rescue a poodle, had vacated his cushion to sneak a peek at Toby's creation.

Toby snapped back to the present. So deeply lost in thought had he been, he'd forgotten both his own whereabouts and Sal's existence. For a while there, he'd been back inside the house in the country, watching as a woman floated towards the nursery. The woman he'd been trying to sketch. With eyes that glowed. At the time he'd felt there was something familiar about her, and that had been confirmed at the dog show.

"I mean, it's almost the same as all yer other masterpieces, like, but it's a good one!" Sal gestured at the walls of Toby's wizard shack. They'd been wallpapered with dozens of similar images. The woman in the house. The woman at the dog show. The more Toby sketched and coloured, the more he knew she was the same woman.

And she was his archnemesis.

The Pointy Woman was back.

The icy, miasmic evil that had stolen Old Joe from his life. She'd murdered his first owner with a perfunctory ease that even now defied Toby's logic. How was it possible to take someone's life without so much as breaking sweat? What could be so wrong with someone that they could do that and feel *nothing*?

"Are you planning on selling them?" Sal asked. "Cos if you are, I've got contacts in the underworld—"

Toby peered down at his chunky rat friend. As long as Toby lived, he hoped he'd never have to venture into Sal's stinky underworld again. Friends or no friends. Sewers were no place for dogs to hang out.

Especially if they weren't that keen on barfs!

"No," he replied, gathering his thoughts at last. "They're not for sale."

"Then, what?" Sal's whiskers twitched. "Oh, I know! An art exhibition!" He bounced away and threw his arms wide. "That's an excellent idea! We can select the best ones—"

Toby shook himself, then lifted his gaze to the images at the very top of the wall. One by one, the pictures started to peel away and float gently to the floor.

"—and once we've settled on those, we can invite folk to come and have a gander—"

Toby started on the next row of images. They

began to scatter around the shack like enormous pieces of confetti.

"We should charge, too. A small exchange." Sal dodged a particularly angry image of the woman with the glowing eyes that had dropped faster than the other versions. "Perhaps we could persuade your lovely neighbour to bake some delectables for the occasion?"

Sal meant Mrs Crouch, the elderly witch who lived next door to Toby and Clarissa in Chamberlain Drive. Mrs Crouch liked to bake, and she loved Toby and his friends, so she kept him well supplied with tasty dog biscuits and snacks. Every few days, she would pop around and refill his old Quality Street tin with fresh treats. Unsurprisingly, since Sal had moved into the shack—albeit only temporarily, apparently—the tin had been denuded of treats more rapidly than usual.

Sal began to gather the fallen images together. "What do you think of black tie and tails?" he asked. "Perhaps Moriarty could be our mistress of ceremonies—she's already eighty per cent there with the black tie and tail bit. Maybe we could find her a dickie bow from somewhere?"

Toby couldn't imagine Moriarty, the black cat from across the road, agreeing to anything as plebeian as donning a *dickie* bow. She'd probably massacre Sal at the mere suggestion.

It wouldn't be pretty.

The walls were almost bare now. Sal had piled the pictures one on top of the other. "It's a shame I can't show my face around town for a bit, cos, heh heh, with all my contacts, getting a bow tie from somewhere would be a piece of cake." He laughed nervously. "I wonder how long it'll be before the Mayflower Lane Mafia forgive me for my trespasses …"

Toby regarded the pile. The newest picture settled gently on top.

"Ya right," Sal exclaimed and swiped at his furry brow. "Probably never. Man, I'm never going to be able to show my face out in public again, am I?"

Toby stared down at the image.

Sal belatedly noticed Toby's lack of engagement. "So, waddayathink?" he asked. "Establish an art gallery or what? We could make a mint."

Toby shook his head. "No."

"No?"

"No art gallery. We're going to burn them."

Sal's eyes widened. "We're going to—? Wait. What?"

"Burn them," said Toby. "Out in the garden."

Sal threw himself on top of the pile. "You can't *burn* them! There's money to be made! Delectables to be enjoyed!"

From outside, the rattle of the back door alerted them to Clarissa's impending arrival. Hurried footsteps, initially almost drowned out by the rain, grew louder until she burst in through the door and shivered, showering them with water droplets. "Gosh, that weather's changed quickly, hasn't it?"

Clarissa Silverwind, Old Joe's granddaughter and Toby's dearly beloved second owner, was wearing her dark hair in two scruffy buns today, her black t-shirt and jeans and her hands spattered with buttermilk paint. For some inexplicable reason she'd decided to engage in some DIY around the house, and that had meant emptying the pantry so she could give it a good clean with the sugar soap and then paint the walls and shelves. She'd spent the previous evening noisily contemplating a new colour scheme for Old Joe's now dated kitchen—Toby hadn't been listening—before settling on buttermilk, lavender and sage but lamenting the fact that she couldn't afford to update the units.

"It's not a great day to be painting." She ruefully rubbed at a spot of paint on her chest. "It'll never dry. I should have taken advantage of our long hot summer. It's properly autumnal today."

"It's going to be wet all day, but it'll be clearing again overnight," Toby informed her. He liked to keep abreast of the latest weather forecasts and had, in fact, been working his way through a weather almanac recently. He'd mentally added weather wizard skills to his 'to be learned' list, but that was an increasingly long list, and he didn't feel like he was making huge strides in any direction. Things kept distracting him from the importance of his education.

Like missing poodles.

And the sudden appearance of zombies.

And stolen puppies.

Clarissa crouched down and gently shooed Sal away from the pile of pictures. Sifting through them, she frowned. "What's this all about, Tobes?"

Toby turned his face away. "Nothing," he said. "A bit of artwork."

"A bit of artwork?" Clarissa flipped over the angry image to show him why she was confused. In this picture, the woman had yellow eyes and the aura surrounding her was a muddy red; the lines of his colouring were spiky and rushed. The woman's nose, sharp and pointed, jutted out of the image, and her mouth sneered with icy contempt. "Is this who I think it is?"

Toby shrugged, miserable that he was lying to Clarissa. Yes, it was more through omission than outright porky pies, but even so, he didn't enjoy it. "That depends on who you think it is." He faked a laugh. "I have an idea that I'm trying to perfect ..."

Clarissa ran a finger down the angry woman's nose. "Hmm. And are any of these perfect?"

"As perfect as they're going to get." Toby levitated the loose felt tip pens back into the mug with the broken handle.

"He wants to burn them!" Sal squeaked indignantly.

Clarissa raised her eyebrows in his direction. She couldn't understand what he was trying to say. Toby had to translate.

"I *am* going to burn them," Toby agreed, his voice firm. "They're full of toxic fury and enchanted malice. By painting them, I bring her back into the world!"

"Ah." Clarissa noted the slip. "It is *her*, then?" She reached over and caressed Toby's face. "This is becoming an obsession, darling."

"I'm never going to forgive her," Toby said.

"I know."

"She doesn't deserve to exist. Not after what she did to Old Joe."

"I know."

"And yet she's back." Toby began to pace. Not that there was a great deal of room to do so in his wizard shack. It was a converted garden shed, after all. "We should revisit the country house, Clarissa."

"Toby, we've been over there half a dozen times in the past week. It's closed up. There's no-one there."

"She's there. I can feel it!" Toby's agitation was beginning to boil over. The atmosphere started to become tense.

Sal, grimacing, decided to scale the bookcase. He'd created a mini hidey-hole on the top shelf.

Clarissa sighed. "This preoccupation you have is worrying me. I don't know how to help you."

Toby jabbed his paw towards the pile of papers Clarissa still held in her hands. They ignited in a flash of flame.

Screeching, Clarissa jumped up and threw them out through the open door into the rain. "Toby!" Smaller pieces of singed paper scattered around the lawn, the edges curling and burning black and orange before melting into ash.

"I apologise," said Toby. "I didn't mean to scare you."

"It's alright." Clarissa breathed out heavily and regarded her spellbound bestie. "Do you need a hug?"

"Probably." Toby allowed her to wrap him in a warm embrace.

"I get it, I do," she murmured into his ear. "But I'm worried about you and the effect that woman has on you. She's no good for your emotional equilibrium."

"That's true," Toby admitted, snuggling in. *But I swear, I intend to be no good for hers either*, he thought. *Before long, she'll be getting her just desserts. I'll see to that.*

Watch this space.

CHAPTER TWO

"Morning, Toby!"

Mrs Crouch, wearing a battered sunhat and peering through a pair of spectacles with bright orange frames that might have been fashionable forty years previously, was trimming back her Rosalia bushes ready for winter.

As Toby had promised, the rain had died away overnight. Today had dawned fine, cool and blustery. The breeze carried a salty tang with it and Toby, pausing, sniffed appreciatively.

"Good morning, Mrs Crouch," he replied. "Thank you for my treats." He said this every time he spotted her. He liked her to know how much he appreciated her. Could you imagine if she decided he was an ungrateful wretch and stopped baking for him?

"You're most welcome, my darling." She smiled. Mrs Crouch was a lady of indeterminate age but must have been in her late seventies, Toby imagined. She was big and bubbly and smiley and cuddly, which were all good things to be. She pulled off her spectacles and squinted down at him. "Are you off on an adventure?"

Toby liked this about his neighbour. She understood him. He still considered his answer carefully, though. Hoomans had a habit of spilling secrets, he'd found. And his business, as we know, was *his* business.

"I thought I'd see if any of my friends are around," he told her, and this wasn't exactly a lie. He was going where he was going, *but* if any of his friends were out and about then that would be all well and good.

"You be careful, then!" Mrs Crouch told him. She didn't need to remind him that Clarissa didn't like him absconding from home without telling her where he was going. She was always scared that he'd be rounded up by the local dog warden and sent back to the pound, but as he kept telling his hooman, dog wardens were pretty much a thing of the past these days. There was no money in the council coffers to pay for them.

"I will!" Toby began to trot away, but a sudden thought occurred to him and he stopped and turned back. "Mrs Crouch?"

Mrs Crouch had replaced her glasses on the end of her nose and was carefully trimming some stems. "Yes, darling?"

"Do you know what number bus goes along the coastal road towards Lyme Regis?"

Mrs Crouch frowned. "Now there's a question." She shook her head. "Now that you mention it, I'm not sure one does. There used to be one that went all the way from Sun Valley to Lyme, but that was back in the day. Way back in the day."

Probably back in the day when your spectacles were fashionable, thought Toby.

"I think nowadays, you have to get the number nine to Seatown and change there."

Hmmm. That sounds complicated, thought Toby.

"Why do you want to go to Lyme?" Mrs Crouch asked, which was a tad nosy of her, to be fair.

"I thought it would be nice to see Mabel," Toby replied. This was a bit of a fib. It *would* be nice to see Mad Mabel, the hedge witch who lived near Lyme Regis—if he could find her, which was sometimes trickier than it sounds because she was a witch with a perfectly decent house who preferred to live in a hedge—but he had no intention of *actually* going there.

No.

But the country house where he'd seen the woman with the glowing eyes? That was en route to Lyme, and a bus would have to pass by the turning. If Clarissa wouldn't take him, he intended to go on his own. He'd considered asking Sal to come along, but two things had stopped him. One: Sal would faint at the first sign of trouble, and two: he wasn't sure what the bus driver would say about a dog *and* a rat trying to clamber aboard their bus for free.

However, taking two buses even by himself would be pushing his luck.

He huffed. "How much would a taxi cost?"

"Money and fair words," Mrs Crouch replied, which Toby took to mean would be expensive. "I rather think you'll have to rely on Clarissa. Is she busy with work?"

"Always," said Toby. Clarissa was a journalist for *The Celestine Times*, contributing regional stories from around the South West. "Not that I mind," he hurriedly added. "I mean, who would? She's enjoying some success, and we can't bee-drudge her that."

"Begrudge," prompted Mrs Crouch. "Although I think I prefer the way you say it." She tittered. "Bee-drudge. I might have to adopt that."

Adopt it? Toby thought. *How do you adopt words?* He'd heard of dogs being adopted. And children. And—ugh—even cats. But words? Too weird. But each to their own. Mrs Crouch was anything but normal.

"I'd better get on," Toby said, but politely.

"Alright. See you later, darling." Still giggling to herself, Mrs Crouch returned to her bush nurturing.

Heart sinking, Toby ambled on. If he couldn't jump on a bus and couldn't afford a taxi, then how would he be able to travel to the house and check whether The Pointy Woman was there or not?

Sighing, he stopped walking. There wasn't a great deal of point in heading into town and hopping on a random bus. He didn't know Seatown and didn't know which bus went from there to Lyme Regis. This was all becoming overly complicated. He needed to formulate a new plan but would only accomplish that with a clear head. And a clear head was not something he'd achieve at home in his wizard shack. Not with Sal there demanding treats or concocting moneymaking schemes.

Better to head for the nearby park, where he could take some deep breaths of fresh air and watch the world go by.

Then ideas would come.

He knew it.

CHAPTER THREE

Toby had made his way to the park. Now he sat on the knobby—and knobbly—trunk of a fallen tree, paws arranged neatly, and practised some meditation.

Ommmmmm.

Ommmmmm.

He stared into himself.

Wouldn't life be simpler if he could only find some forgiveness for Miranda Dervish, The Pointy Woman? Didn't everyone deserve a modicum of compassion? Perhaps she had achieved many good things in her life and earned a few brownie points along the way.

Perhaps she had children who adored her, and she them.

Perhaps she kept homing pigeons and they returned to her whenever she set them free, simply thanks to the magnitude of her love for them.

Perhaps ... Toby scrunched up his nose, meditating as hard as he could ... the plants in her living room were vibrant and green and—

ARGH! He couldn't do it anymore.

Old Joe's sweet, smiling face interrupted the flow, and Toby almost choked on the venom simmering inside.

Miranda Dervish wasn't some kind and benevolent middle-aged woman doting on grandchildren, pets and plants. She was a cold, conniving murderer on an evil power trip. She would destroy anyone who placed obstacles in her path.

All this time, thought Toby, *I've been working hard at improving my wizarding skills. A little knowledge goes a long way. And yet ...*

He sighed and squeezed his eyes tighter, willing a sense of calm to replace the dread and anxiety that bubbled immediately below the surface.

And yet ... if there was a single crucial and profound thing he'd learned, it was that no matter how hard you worked and how hard you studied, you would only ever scratch the surface of the massive mountain of knowledge that existed. What he knew

—what *little* he knew—he doubted was enough to bring The Pointy Woman down.

He opened his eyes ...

... and nearly fell off his tree stump.

Two feet away, a tall goose with a slender black neck and piercing eyes was staring at him.

"I know you, don't I?" asked the goose.

Toby shook off his malaise and forced a smile. "Probably!" he replied cheerily. "I come here all the time with my hooman. You can't miss her. She's one of those emo-goths with pigtails and a pale face."

The goose arched an eyebrow. Not that he even *had* properly defined eyebrows, but you could imagine where they were. A bit like an influencer on TokTik. "Fairly sure you're the dude who was disturbing our sleep not so long ago. With the poodle."

"Ah." Toby nodded. "Well remembered. Would it help if I apologised?"

"Got any bread?" the goose demanded.

"Bread?" Toby frowned.

"Are you hard of hearing, or what? Do you have any bread? Toast? Crumpet? Teacake? Hot cross bun?"

"Hot cross buns are a bit out of season," Toby pointed out.

The goose ignored him. "Any or all of the above?"

"I'm all out of snacks," Toby told the goose, somewhat regretfully. In his case, a cheese straw would not have gone amiss at this moment in time. "But the next time I come for a walk, I'll—"

The goose hissed, jabbing its head forward.

Toby leaned back. "Whoa there, tiger. You do know there are signs telling people not to feed you bread products?" he asked.

"Signs?" The goose squinted towards the fairly sizable pond that locals euphemistically called Swan Lake.

"Those yellow things with writing on?"

The goose sneered. "I can't read."

"Right." Toby nodded. "Gotcha. Well, if you ever need someone to read for you, I'm your dog." He hopped off his perch. "In fact, to compensate for disturbing your sleep that *one* night a few *long* weeks ago now, why don't I come over and read you a bedtime story?"

The goose hissed again.

"No, seriously, there are some fantastic fairy tales out there." He trotted sideways away from the goose so it couldn't lunge at him. "It's a date!" he yelled and turned tail. Giggling, he pelted along the path that led deeper into the park—where there were fewer children, and dog owners were allowed off their leads while their dogs socialised.

Toby exchanged peemails with a few friends and sniffed a few backsides. He wagged his tail at some of the hoomans he knew, raced around with a young whippet—who evidently recognised him as some distant kin—inspected the contents of an upended bin along with a labradoodle and a Saluki-cross-something-with-short-legs, exchanged the latest gossip with a visually impaired Staffy and then, alone once more, began to loop back towards Swan Lake.

The canine contact had cheered him up.

You see, he told himself as he trotted along, tail high and wagging back and forth in rhythm with his step, *I'm a dog first and a wizard second, and life* ***doesn't*** *have to be complicated.*

An old man sitting on a bench chuckled as Toby passed by. "You're looking cheerful, lad!"

Toby paused and gazed back at the man. A similar age to Old Joe before he died, the man was wearing a lightweight, slightly grubby raincoat over a hand-knitted jumper, casual trousers and worn leather shoes. A woven shopping bag had been placed on the bench beside him, along with a newspaper.

An *actual* paper copy of a newspaper.

How remarkably old school.

Clarissa would appreciate that.

"I've been having fun with my friends," Toby admitted. "Have a lovely day!" He stepped away, giving his tail an extra wag.

"I miss having friends," the old fellow said, sounding mournful.

Toby halted in surprise. Cautiously, he turned back. "What happened to them?" he asked.

"Some married and moved away. Some had children and became busy. Some died." The man shrugged. "You have fewer as you get older. People tend to drift apart." He nodded at Toby. "Does that happen with dogs?"

Toby considered this. He'd wanted to pop in to see his friend Pickle at Sweet Pea's Parlour for Pampered Pooches, but Pea had yet to reopen. Perhaps she never would. Added to this, he hadn't seen his bestie Pippin for a few weeks, that much was true. "Maybe," he said.

"It's sad." The old man sighed and reached into his shopping bag. Drawing out a Tupperware box, he flipped the lid. His nails were neatly trimmed with beautiful half-moons. Clarissa would be jealous. Her nails were generally ragged. If she painted them—always black, midnight blue or aubergine—they chipped almost instantaneously because she was constantly tapping away on her keyboard.

Toby watched as the man began to peel a satsuma, noticing his swollen knuckles and the slight twist of some of his digits. Poor chap had a touch of arthritis by the look of it.

"I don't suppose you like orange, do you?" the man asked, dropping his peelings into the Tupperware box.

Toby, who had learned never to accept treats from strangers, wrinkled his nose. He did, in fact, like oranges. Unsurprisingly, there wasn't much he didn't like. "No, thank you."

"What about my sandwich crusts?" the man asked.

"What flavour?" The response burst out of Toby's mouth before he could think.

"Cheese," the man said.

Toby drooled. "Cheese is my favourite favourite."

The man held out a corner. Toby could see grated cheese sandwiched between the slices of bread. "No, thank you," he repeated, although he doubted his stomach would ever forgive him.

The man's face fell. "No? Okay. I can give feed them to the geese or the swans—"

"It does say not to feed the birds with bread." Toby couldn't help pointing this out again.

"You can read, can you?" The old man perked up at this. "You're an incredibly gifted dog."

Toby edged closer. Time to state the obvious. "You can understand me."

The man nodded. "Loud and clear."

"Are you a wizard?" Toby asked.

The man hesitated, pressing his lips together.

"Or a witch? Or something similar?" Toby pressed.

Finally, the old chap nodded.

"I was a wizard," he admitted. "I'm not now. Not anymore."

"Wow!" Toby beamed. "I'm training to be a wizard, you know?"

The man laughed. "I'm sure you'll be marvellous!"

"That's my intention." Toby came closer to the bench and held out his paw. "I'm Toby," he said. "Toby Silverwind."

The old man started and stared down with

watery blue eyes. "Silverwind, you say? That's a blast from the past." He collected himself. "I'm Rory Elmdytch."

"Pleased to meet you, Wizard Elmdytch," said Toby.

The old fellow chuckled. "Rory is fine with me."

Toby, keen to find out more about Rory's reaction to his name, pressed on. "Did you know my hooman? Old Joe?"

"Joseph Silverwind? I most certainly did. He was my coven leader for a fair few years. A truly lovely man and a wonderful wizard."

"Oh." Toby melted inside.

"Is Joe still with us?" Rory peered about, as though expecting Old Joe to come walking along the path clutching a lead and wagging a finger at his rogue dog.

"You didn't hear?" Toby's sigh was heartfelt. "I hate to have to tell you ... but Old Joe died."

"Goodness. I'm sorry to hear that, lad." Rory leaned forward and gently smoothed Toby's head. "Another good one gone. Who looks after you now?"

"Old Joe's granddaughter, Clarissa. She's pawesome."

Rory laughed softly. "I'm glad to hear that at least."

"I look after her, mostly," Toby corrected him. "She's always getting us into scrapes."

"Is she now? Good for her." Rory regarded Toby shrewdly.

Toby affected an air of complete innocence and changed the subject. "I've never seen you here before. I don't think." There was a chance they'd missed each other, he supposed, or that Toby simply hadn't noticed him sitting here alone on a bench.

"Truth to tell, I rarely visit the park anymore," Rory told him. "But autumn is here and it won't be long till winter, and there probably aren't that many days of sunshine left in my life. I wanted to make the most of this fine day."

Awwww. Toby thawed a little more. "And you met me!" he beamed. "So that's a bonus!"

"It certainly is!" Rory laughed out loud and pushed himself off the bench, taking his time to pack away his lunchbox and his newspaper.

Toby regretted that he hadn't shared the cheese sammich after all. What a waste.

"May I accompany you to the gate?" Toby asked politely.

"That would be lovely of you," Rory said. They walked side by side, Rory taking it slowly, Toby matching his pace. They exchanged small talk—Rory remarking on various dogs they passed and Toby telling him their names—until finally they made it to the gates.

"It's been lovely to spend time in your company today, Toby," Rory said.

"And me with you. I'll be sure to tell Clarissa about you, and we'll look out for you the next time we walk in the park on a sunny day!" Toby promised.

"I'll look forward to it. Farewell," said Rory, bowing his head.

Toby bowed his furry crown in response and began to walk towards the crossing.

"Toby?" Rory called him back. Toby returned and gazed at the old man. "This is going to perhaps sound ... crazy ..." Rory cocked his head, frowning. "I don't do magick anymore. I don't ... do much ... but—ugh." He shook his head. "I get a feeling that something ..." He stamped his foot. It wasn't an effective stamp, given that his old body lacked the movement of a younger man, but it successfully carried his emotion across. "Darn it!"

Toby waited patiently, his brown eyes soft.

Rory started again. "Something happened to Joe, didn't it? Something awful?"

"Yes." Toby studied his paws for a moment

before lifting his head. "He was killed by someone who wanted to access a secret."

"I see." Rory scratched his forehead. "But you thwarted that person."

Toby was impressed. Rory was a seer. "Yes."

Rory smiled, but his face was pale. "Well done, lad."

Toby couldn't help himself. "But she managed to get away, and I didn't get to bring her to justice. Not yet."

"Her?" Rory repeated, and his voice sounded strangely hollow. "Who was she?"

"Miranda Dervish," Toby told him.

Rory swayed sharply backwards, almost as though he'd been slapped.

"Do you know her?" Toby asked.

"No," Rory said, his already pale face turned ashen.

"Then—" Toby started, intending to ask why Rory had reacted that way.

But Rory had lurched away. "Take care, young 'un," he called.

"Rory?" Toby barked after him. "Wizard Elmdytch?"

But Rory continued to shuffle away and didn't once glance back.

CHAPTER FOUR

"You look like you've lost a shilling and found a sixpence," Moriarty called over to him.

Toby, sitting on the kerb in front of thirty-three Chamberlain Drive, knitted his eyebrows together. "Is there a specific look for people who find sixpences?" he asked.

"It's a figure of speech," Moriarty told him, strolling over from her side of the road.

"Sixpences are fairly rare these days, aren't they?" Toby asked. "I imagine if I found one, I'd look totally thrilled!"

"We've a jam jar full of them in my house," Moriarty told him. "The lady hooman works in a shop and people try to fob them off as modern fivepences, apparently. So she collects them."

Toby couldn't help but be impressed by this. "You could be rich!" he exclaimed.

Moriarty dismissed the idea out of hand. "I don't think they're worth anything. If they were, we wouldn't be living here, would we?" She sniffed disdainfully and directed her gaze down the road to where three children were speeding around on bicycles, throwing themselves on and off the pavement and attempting to jump obstacles, all the while screeching loudly. The eldest of them, a boy aged eight or so with sandy-coloured hair, was showing off to the younger girl and boy, who Toby recognised as his siblings. The youngest—a chubby-cheeked boy of about four—still had the stabilisers on his bicycle.

"You don't like children?" Toby asked.

"In my opinion, they're unnecessary," said Moriarty. "Unnecessarily messy. Unnecessarily noisy. Unnecessarily demanding. Unnecessarily sticky. Unnecessarily existent."

"Harsh," said Toby, although given the amount of noise these three sprogs were making, he found himself somewhat sympathetic to Moriarty's point of view. He wasn't entirely sure they should have been playing in the road though. Chamberlain Drive was a quiet street, but traffic travelled along it in both directions. "Let's hope they don't get *unnecessarily* squished."

"*C'est la vie*." Moriarty shrugged.

Toby raised his prize-winning eyebrows but kept schtum. He could never be sure exactly how evil Moriarty was. She was his friend. That was mostly all that mattered to him.

"Tell me, oh wise one," Moriarty mocked. "What *is* the matter with you this afternoon? Didn't your hooman offer you lunch?"

"I only eat twice a day." Toby felt the need to point this out. "Breakfast and dinner." *Snacks don't count*, he reminded himself.

"So?" Moriarty doggedly persisted. "What then?"

Toby sighed and collapsed onto his haunches. "I've a lot on my mind."

"Is this about that wretched elbowy woman?" Moriarty asked. "The one who killed your old hooman?"

Toby corrected her. "The Pointy Woman. And yes."

"Ha! Want me to scratch her eyes out for you?"

Toby smirked. "Be my guest. If I ever find her." He huffed.

"I thought she was at that house in the country

you were telling me about." Toby had recounted his last adventure to Moriarty at her eager request. They enjoyed chilling on the roof of Toby's wizard shack, sharing gossip and shooting the breeze together. There wasn't much Toby hadn't confided to her. Even though she was a cat.

Toby nodded. "I genuinely, truly, honestly believe she is."

"That's good enough for me. What are we waiting for, then?"

"I have transportation issues," Toby lamented. "Clarissa is refusing to take me anymore because she thinks it's a waste of time—"

"To be fair, you have been travelling out there a lot," Moriarty said.

Toby's eyes widened. "Have you been *spying* on us?"

"Of course. What else do you think I'm doing when I'm lounging in the window?"

"Sunbathing?"

"My fur can't get any darker."

"Napping? That's what I'd do." Toby couldn't physically fit on his windowsill. Not easily, anyway. Sometimes he tried, but he tended to lose his balance if he moved in his sleep.

"Occasionally," Moriarty admitted. "Why don't you stow away on a bus?"

"I could try that. But it's two buses and I'd have to change in Seatown, so that worries me a bit."

Moriarty looked stumped. "I see the problem."

They watched the children again. Round and round and round they went, narrowly missing the wing mirror of a passing Hyundai.

"What about that chap who comes around?" Moriarty asked, turning her head to watch the Hyundai pass them.

"DC Ed?" Toby asked. Detective Constable Ed Plum and Clarissa were seeing a lot of each other now they were—*snigger*—boyfriend and girlfriend. *Eww*. "I doubt Clarissa would let him. Besides, I can't communicate with him. That is—" He corrected himself. "*I* can obviously communicate perfectly well, it's only that DC Ed can't understand a word I say. He's useless."

Moriarty giggled. "Communication isn't effective unless both parties understand each other."

"Wow," said Toby. "Have you been reading a dictionary? I thought I was the only animal that did that."

"No. I don't read. I've been at home for too many

office Zoom calls with the male hooman, though." She rolled her eyes. "So deeply dreary."

A child shrieked. A different kind of shriek to all the previous ones. They had been high-octane excitement and mischief mingled with the exhilaration of freedom and youth. This one sounded fearful. It was swiftly followed by a crash and a thud.

Both Toby and Moriarty cowered and winced at the same time. When Toby peeked, the littlest child lay sprawled on the pavement on Toby's side of the road, directly in front of Mrs Crouch's house.

"Muuuuuuuuuuuuuuuuuuuum!" yelled the eldest boy.

The girl abandoned her bicycle and made a dash for their house across the road. "Muuu-uuuu-uuuum?" she called. "Mum? Mason's fallen off his bike!"

"Do you think we should help?" Toby jumped to his paws.

Moriarty pulled a face. "Probably best if we don't get involved. You know what hoomans are like when animals are anywhere near their precious offspring."

She had a point. It didn't matter anyway because Mum was already on her way. Dressed in shorts and slippers, her hair tied back with a scarf, and wearing a pair of bright yellow Marigold gloves, she sped across the road. "Mason?" she bellowed. "Ohmilord! Someone call an ambulance! Mason?"

Mason picked that moment to open his eyes and goggle at his mother. He rather reminded Toby of Sal at that moment: the way his ratty friend fainted at the first hint of trouble but came miraculously back to life as soon as the danger had passed.

Mason took a deep breath and then screamed at the top of his lungs.

"Poor kid. He must be dying," said Toby, leaning away from the noise. "Rest in peace."

Moriarty covered her ears. "Is he heck as like. Nobody dies that loudly."

One or two of their neighbours had come out to see what all the commotion was about. Mr Dawlish, a middle-aged ex-soldier who lived at number twenty-seven, next door but one to Mrs Crouch, knelt beside Mason and his mother and gave the boy a quick once-over. He couldn't have found anything seriously wrong, because almost immediately he was hoisting Mason onto his shoulder and carrying him over the road, Mum and siblings trailing in his wake. They went inside and closed the door. The other neighbours dispersed.

That was the end of that excitement.

Moriarty examined her left paw. "Now's your chance," she said.

"Huh?" Toby didn't have a clue what she meant.

"The bicycle."

Toby, perplexed, peered down the road, to where Mason's bike lay on its side. "What about it?"

"You had a transportation issue, right?" Moriarty reminded him.

"Ye-eeeeeeees." Where was she going with this?

She smiled, her eyes glistening with mischief. "Well, now you don't."

Toby guffawed. Moriarty was officially crazy. "I can't ride a bicycle!"

"How hard can it be?" Moriarty asked. "If a hooman can do it, you can do it. After all, they only have two legs and you have four."

Toby studied the bicycle askance. Moriarty had a point. He made his way slowly over to it and sniffed it suspiciously. As you'd expect, given that it belonged to a four-year-old, the bike was on the small side. It was red with a silver streak. The graphic splayed across the top tube declared *Lightning Bolt!*, which Toby assumed must be its name.

It didn't look like a lightning bolt. In fact, it didn't look like much close-up. He nudged the pedal. It rotated. The back wheel started to move.

Interesting.

He nudged the pedal again. And again. By making the pedal turn faster, he could make the wheel spin faster.

These, then, were the mechanics of a bicycle. Stealing a quick look around to make sure none of his neighbours was about, he nodded at the machine. "*Consurge*!" he ordered, and the bicycle righted itself.

Moriarty nodded her approval. "Now you're cooking on gas!"

This had to be one of Moriarty's odd sayings, Toby decided, because clearly he wasn't cooking at all, let alone on gas. "Help me get it back to my house," he said.

"I think not!" Moriarty recoiled in horror. "What do you think I am? A removal woman?"

"Please? I can't do it on my own," Toby pleaded.

"Of course you can." Moriarty's swift response was waspish. "You're the great wizard, remember?"

CHAPTER FIVE

You'd have thought that great wizards would not find it too difficult to master the art of riding a bicycle. However, no matter how Toby tried, he could not grasp the relationship between balance, pedalling and steering. He howled in frustration as he slipped off for the umpteenth time in twenty minutes.

"Oopsie," said Sal, sitting on the garden wall, watching proceedings.

"You shouldn't talk with your mouth full," Toby remarked crossly. "Where did you get that cheese from anyway?"

"What, this old thing?" Sal held out a lump of Cheddar as big as his head and almost as furry.

"From behind the washing machine at number twelve."

"Gross," said Toby, a tad snootily. They both knew full well that Toby would have swallowed it down without a second thought.

"Number twenty-three chucked out a whole kweesh the other night," Sal told him. "And there was only a speck of mould on it."

"Don't we feed you enough?" Toby asked. Clarissa hadn't been overly keen when she found out that Sal had taken up residence in the wizard shack, but she wasn't one to make too much of a fuss about such things. To that end, she provided Sal with a decent amount of sustenance in his own rat-sized bowl that she'd bought from the pet shop downtown.

"When is enough e-*nough*?" Sal asked, and Toby couldn't find fault with that.

He climbed back onto the Lightning Bolt. Part of the problem was that his legs struggled to meet the pedals, even if the bike was designed for a four-year-old. A toddler's trike might have been a better bet. In addition, he didn't have feet, only paws, so the surface area pushing down on the pedals was severely restricted.

Toby pushed down through his left hind leg. The Lightning Bolt shifted forward. And down with his right. Again, the bike lurched forward. *And down,* thought Toby, powering his left leg. *And down!* With his right. *Down! Down! Down! Oh, my dogness!*

The bike rolled smoothly along the patio as Toby found a rhythm.

Down! Down! Down!

He altered his weight and, using his right paw, steered around to the right. "Woohooo!" he shouted.

And down! Down! Down!

Building up speed, he cycled back to where he started. The wind blew at his ears, making them flap. "Yeeha!"

And around he went again, pumping the pedals, working the rhythm despite the unfamiliar ache in his hind legs.

The back door opened and Clarissa emerged. Her forehead creased in surprise. "Toby?"

"I'm cycling!" he announced, bobbing his head with excitement.

"Oh my life!" Clarissa clamped her hands to her chest.

"It's fine!" shouted Toby. Except suddenly it wasn't. Because it occurred to him that he needed to slow down and stop but, even when he stopped pedalling, the bicycle carried on, and because he'd stopped pedalling, for some reason he'd also stopped steering, and one of the garden's retaining walls was far too close, and—

"Eurgh!" Toby yelped—not sounding all that different from poor old Mason earlier—closing his eyes as the wall loomed in front of him. Unfortunately, the bike hit the raised edge of the patio first and Toby was catapulted into the air. He flew over the retaining wall, landing chin first on a paved seating area, skidding along the slabs until finally coming to rest.

He lay there winded for a long moment until finally Clarissa unclamped her hands and whispered, "Toby? Are you alive?"

"Yeth," said Toby, his tongue oddly thick and useless.

Sal had abandoned his cheese and hurried to Toby's side. Now he flicked one of Toby's eyelids open and examined his pupils. "The lights are on but there's no-one home," he rasped.

"I'm home." Toby groaned. He wasn't sure he could move.

Clarissa joined them and hurriedly felt along his spine. "Can you feel me touching you?" she asked.

"Of courth," said Toby.

"Can you stand up?" Clarissa asked, her voice laden with panic.

"Do I hath to?" Toby wanted to know.

Clarissa pulled at his shoulders. "Come on, baby. Up you get."

Reluctantly, Toby did as she asked, his muscles screaming, his bones cricking with discontent. He turned his head to look at Clarissa. "Oh no! Oh no!" she squealed. "You're bleeding!"

"Am I?" Toby peered down at himself. All he could see was his chest and his front paws and they looked fine, but with his head tipped down, he couldn't fail to spot the drop of blood that suddenly dripped onto the sand-coloured slab below and bloomed bright. "Yeurgh!"

"Ewww." Sal grimaced.

"Let me see! Let me see!" Clarissa's panic obliged her to repeat everything she said. Her breath came in short, sharp bursts as she pulled Toby's head to her lap to get a better look. "What have you done? What have you done?" She pulled open Toby's mouth and looked inside. "Oh dear, oh dear! I'll have to call the vet! I'll have to—"

"No." Toby pulled himself free. "I'm thine."

"You're not fine. You might need stitches!" Clarissa argued.

"Ohhhh." Sal dropped into a swoon.

Toby rolled his eyes. "Thorter," he said.

"Pardon?" Clarissa asked, her eyes filled with tears.

"Thorter," Toby repeated. "Can I pleath have thome thorter?"

"Water." Clarissa's laugh was high pitched. "Yes. Water. Water." She hurried away through the back door, returning before Toby had had time to slide back down onto the paving slabs for a rest.

He drank a little, trying the cool liquid out in his mouth. His tongue felt fat and a bit defective, and it had started to smart, but the water went down easily enough and he almost drained the bowl.

"Let me see now," Clarissa demanded, and Toby dutifully allowed her to peer into his mouth and check his head over. "I think you'll be okay," she said, sounding relieved but cautious. "It looks like you've bitten your tongue, but the bleeding is already stopping—"

"That'th good."

"And scraped your chin, but again, I think you'll be alright."

"Maybe a thort nap and a thammich?" Toby suggested.

Clarissa breathed out in amused exasperation. "How can you think of your stomach at a time like this?"

"My thtomach ith thine. It'th my chin and my thongue. You thaid tho!"

"Come on then. Inthide." Clarissa made a choking noise. "What the—I mean *inside*! Crikey. You've got me doing it now."

"Oopth." Toby giggled.

She reached down to pick up the water bowl.

"Wait!" Toby doghandled the water bowl magickly. "Come on, Thal!" he said, levitating it, turning it upside down and sprinkling the remains of the water over his teeny friend.

Sal jerked upright. "I'm drowning!" he shrieked.

"No. It wath jutht me. We're going indoorth."

"Good heavens!" Sal shook water droplets from his coat. "I thought I was being waterboarded."

"Not at all," Toby told him. "I thave that for my enemyth."

"Pity The Pointy Woman then," muttered Sal, and followed Clarissa and Toby back into the house.

"Do you want to tell me what you were doing?" Clarissa asked a little later. She'd opted to run a warm bath for Toby—against his wishes—in order to clean him thoroughly and so she could get a better look at all his scrapes, bumps and bruises. Now, she carefully parted his fur to check for wounds. Apart from his tongue and chin, and some swelling around his lip, everything seemed superficial.

Thankfully.

Not particularly, thought Toby, fighting to summon a little carefree joviality. Truth was, he'd started feeling a bit achy now that the shock had ebbed away. "I wanted to learn to ride a bithycle," he said, forcing himself to appear brighter.

"You were doing so well," said Sal, perched on the edge of the bath and rubbing his chunk of soapy sponge into his crevices. Sal adored bathtime. He couldn't get enough of smelling like Mrs Crouch's flower garden.

So much better than smelling like a sewer.

"I almotht had it," Toby agreed.

"Maybe you should have tried applying the brakes," Clarissa suggested.

"There are braketh?" Toby found himself stupefied at this news. "On a bithycle?"

"Of course!" Clarissa laughed. "Didn't you know?"

"No." *Obviouthly!*

"They're on the handlebars. You pull the lever."

Clarissa began to gently massage Toby's chest with the soap. It felt sooooooooooo good.

"I wondered what they were for," Toby admitted. "Oh well. Nectht time."

Clarissa made a strangled noise in her throat. "Please don't let there be a next time."

"May I have more soap, please?" Sal asked, holding out his sponge and, while Clarissa didn't understand what he was saying, she understood the gesture and provided a blob of soapy goo where he directed. "Coo!"

"You must be the cleanest rat in the known universe," Clarissa remarked.

"I'll have to have another go," Toby argued. "I'm thure I can mathter riding a bithycle."

A sudden thought struck Clarissa. "Where did you get it from?"

Uh-oh. "Where did I get what from?" Toby feigned innocence.

"You know exactly what I'm talking about." Clarissa narrowed her eyes. "The bicycle! Where did you get it from?"

"Erm ... locally ..." Toby grimaced inwardly.

Clarissa sat back on her haunches, rubbing her back. Leaning over the tub tended to give her backache. "Oh, Toby! Tell me you didn't *steal* it!"

"I didn't thteal it!" *Did I? Oh dear.* "I ... I borrowed it!"

"That amounts to the same thing."

"It doethn't at all!"

"It absolutely does." Clarissa sighed. "Where exactly did you get it from?"

Toby sighed, his shoulders drooping. Bang went his great transportation plan. "Thome kid called Mathon at number twenty-thicth."

"Fine." Clarissa pulled the plug, turned the shower on and, after checking the temperature of the water, directed the hose towards Toby's back. "I'll return it. I hope there isn't any damage to it—"

"There'th more damage to me, to be fair." Toby hung his head.

"Awwww. Poor love." Clarissa finished rinsing him off and nodded at Sal, who slid down the side of the bath and stood under the spray, paws raised like a water-worshipping sea otter or something of that kind.

As she wrapped Toby in a towel and hugged him, it occurred to her to ask, "Why did you want to ride a bicycle in the first place?"

Toby could have styled it out, perhaps, with a cheery, 'Well, why not?' but all of the fight had escaped through his chin and his tongue. For now, at least. “I thought I could ride it over to the houth.” He didn’t need to clarify *which* house.

Clarissa became still. She remained silent for a while. Sal, still waiting to be dried off, dripped into the bath. Eventually Toby lifted his head and regarded Clarissa with some concern. *Is there anyone there?* he wondered.

Clarissa bit her lip. “I don’t want you going there by yourself,” she said.

“But you thaid the’th not there!”

“She’s *not* there! But it’s a busy road—”

“I know the’th there!”

“Toby!”

“Clariitha!”

“You can’t be—”

“The’th there, and you knowth I know that—”

“But—”

“I think the’ll come after uth unleth we go athter her thirtht!”

“You can’t know for certain that the woman you saw at the house—”

“And at the dog thow—”

“—and at the dog show was Miranda Dervish.”

“Aooooooo!” Toby lifted his head and howled. Days—and nights—of frustration bubbled over. Sal tried to dive for cover but there was none to be had.

He slipped and slithered around the bathtub in a panic. Clarissa, startled by Toby's reaction, made a grab for the rat and placed him safely on the bath mat. Sal didn't stay there long. He hurried behind Clarissa and hid behind the sink pedestal.

"Toby!" Clarissa spluttered in alarm. "Calm down, babe!"

"Aaaaaoooooooo-oooo!"

"Okay, okay. You're okay!"

Clarissa lifted him and the towel out of the bath and set him on her lap. "Gosh, you're shaking! You're okay," she said again. "I promise nothing—and no-one—will hurt you!"

"Aaaaoooooooo!" Toby cried, his nose pointing at the ceiling. *She doesn't get it!* he thought. *It's not me I'm worried about. What if The Pointy Woman gets to Clarissa? Or Ed? Or Mrs Crouch? Or even—dog help me—Sal? I can't let her destroy everything I care about!*

Tears shone in Clarissa's eyes. "Toby? Toby? What is it? Are you in pain?"

"In my thoul." He sniffed.

Clarissa relaxed a little. If the snark was back, so was her boy. She smoothed his head. "What can I do to help you?"

"Take me back to the houth—"

Clarissa frowned. "Toby—"

"Otherwithe I'm going to thteal another bithycle."

"Arrgh!" Clarissa closed her eyes. When she opened them again, she sighed. "Alright. I'll take you once more. Note the *once*! And that will be an end to it!"

CHAPTER SIX

The following morning found Toby and Clarissa in the car bright and early.

Or rather, Clarissa was bright and it was definitely early, but Toby felt like he'd been hit by a truck. His chin hurt, his tongue hurt, his chest hurt and his back legs hurt. In fact, the only things that didn't ache were his ears, but he was sure that Clarissa would soon put paid to that.

In the interests of getting as much work done as possible later in the day, Clarissa had insisted they leave home by seven in the morning. It was now ten past, and Toby had managed to limp to the car—exaggerating his infirmity more than strictly necessary—when Clarissa finally made it out of the front door armed with a bobble hat—black with a white

Nightmare Before Christmas smiley face—and a travel mug containing her coffee. Clarissa wasn't a huge fan of caffeine, but she did occasionally drink one in the morning to get her going, especially after a late night or a heavy session.

"Are we going to be doing a stakeout?" Toby asked as Clarissa jumped into the driver's seat. At least his lisp had eased overnight, that was something.

"I shouldn't have thought so, but I figured if you wanted to have a good sniff around, that would take care of your morning walk and I could kill two birds with one stone while checking the email on my phone." Clarissa smiled triumphantly and pulled her hat on.

"I see."

"Clunk, click." Clarissa reached over and belted Toby in. "We don't want you faceplanting the windscreen today, do we?"

"No," Toby agreed. "Although, it would be unlikely to happen. Not sure whether you know where the brakes are anyway."

"Oh, ho ho." Clarissa did her own seatbelt up. "You must be feeling better. At least I know where they are on a *bithycle*!" She giggled and started the car.

"It's cruel to take the mickey out of me," Toby complained, but he couldn't help chuckling along with her.

They drove in silence for a while, listening to the music on the radio. The outside world was only now beginning to wake up. The sun hadn't been up for long, and a damp mist lingered on the ground. If the sun came out—and that was a big if today because rain was forecast—then it would quickly burn off the mist, otherwise they were likely to see a dank, drizzly autumn day.

Traffic was light as they headed out of town. It was a school day but the school run had yet to properly get going. They rounded a bend and climbed a hill—and there, to their right, they could see the sea. The water reflected the sky: grey and ominous.

They kept climbing and kept taking the bends—too slowly for Toby's liking at times, but it might have helped if Clarissa had changed down the gears—round to the left and round to the right like some dystopian roller coaster. The Romans could never have reached this part of East Devon, that was for certain, because if they had, they'd never have left the roads so curly-wurly.

They missed out, thought Toby. Even on a grey day like today, the forests to his left pulsed with life, and the sheer diversity of the landscape filled him with joy. He drifted into his mind, vibing on green fields and forests and the tangle of autumn bramble.

They drove for approximately twenty minutes before arriving at the turn to the lane that would lead them to the house. Clarissa pulling hard on the steering wheel had the result of flinging Toby to his left and breaking his blissed-out spell of peace.

Time to get with it, he told himself. Straining at the seatbelt, he used his front paws to balance against the dashboard. Clarissa's battered old car thunked and jolted along the lane—it was one of those tracks where the grass grows along the centre because it is so rarely used—carelessly throwing the occupants up to the roof and back down into their seats.

"Yoikes! Ouch!" Clarissa grumbled as she smacked her head twice in quick succession. "Ooy-ah!" And again.

"I never thought I'd say this, but if you slow down a bit more—" Toby began to suggest.

"Who's driving here, buster? Me or you?" Clarissa sniped and, before he could reply, added, "We all saw the results of your driving yesterday."

She's never going to let me forget it, is she? "How about you slip into second gear?" Toby suggested. "Or even first," he added under his breath. Not that he knew anything about gears particularly, but it was something that Not-so-dead-to-me Ed had a habit of saying—in a calm-yet-oddly-panicked voice—when Clarissa was approaching roundabouts and junctions.

"When I want your advice—OOH!" The car hit a pothole, clunked and jumped a foot into the air.

Clarissa slowed down and changed gear. The engine whined as they followed the lane slowly upwards, but it was altogether more comfortable than before. Toby was glad—for the sake of his poor tongue and aching bones, if nothing else.

"This wasn't here before." Clarissa came to a stop and pulled on the handbrake.

Toby stared out of the front window. A brand-new gate, the wood still creamy fresh, blocked their way. "There's a sign on it." Before Clarissa could say no, Toby unclipped his belt and opened the door. He bounded out, landing on the grassy verge with a grunt. "Owwww, my joints!"

Clarissa followed, the car idling behind them seeming loud in the otherwise still surroundings. "I'm fairly sure we could have read it from inside the car," Clarissa said.

Toby didn't care. He wanted a close-up. "Blackwell Manor. Private Property. Strictly No Admittance," he read.

"And there you are." Clarissa shrugged.

"That means someone's living here," Toby reminded her.

"Not necessarily. There might ... I mean ... there could be property developers ..." Clarissa sounded as though she was going to bluster some excuse or other, but she gazed around and shivered visibly. "This is a weird place," she admitted.

Toby peered through the slats in the fence. "There are fresh tyre tracks on the other side."

"Have you noticed there aren't any birds singing?" Clarissa asked, wrapping her arms around herself. "That's unusual, right?"

"If you'll allow me to slip through the fence I can go and take a look," Toby told her.

She glared down at him. "Absolutely not."

Toby rolled his eyes. "According to you, The Pointy Woman doesn't live here. *Nobody* lives here. Therefore, there can't be anything to worry about!"

"I know I said that, but ..." Clarissa trailed off, her eyes sweeping the land around them, searching among the trees and the hedgerows, cocking her head to listen for the faintest noise.

"If there's something wrong here, I want to find out," Toby insisted. "I'll be quick."

"No." Clarissa shook her head, and now she'd turned pale, paler than normal. "You can't go. Not ..." She heaved out a sigh. "Not alone."

"You're coming with me?" Toby didn't like that idea any more than Clarissa liked the idea of him going off alone.

"Let me move the car. There was a passing place further down. I'll reverse it down there." She hopped into the battered old Nissan before half climbing out again, one leg on the track, one inside. "Stay. There! Do. NOT. Move. An. Inch."

"Okay. Chill." Toby hunkered down to wait. Clarissa slipped the gear into reverse. The car whined as she allowed it to roll down the hill, only occasionally having to brake and manoeuvre. Truth to tell, she was almost better at reversing than she was at driving forwards.

Toby lost sight of her around a bend. A moment later, the engine stopped.

He waited patiently until, finally, she returned. She nodded at him—"Let's go"—before gently shepherding him towards the gate.

"Ow," he grumbled as he squeezed through the

gap, wishing he could be a little more cat and a little less wounded canine.

Clarissa climbed over the gate with ease and, together, they followed the track towards the house, glad of the cover that the trees, overgrown hedges and tall grass provided them. Finally, they caught their first glimpse of the mansion.

Clarissa sidestepped into a clump of bushes. "Pssst!" She beckoned for Toby to follow her in.

"What are you doing?" he asked.

She crouched down, her hat getting snagged on a branch. Rescuing it and pulling it back down over her hair, she whispered, "I think we should try a spot of surveillance from a distance."

"I see." Toby sat down beside her.

"Shame I didn't bring my coffee."

"I could go back and get it if you like?" Toby offered, uncertain whether Clarissa was cut out to be a spy. Did James Bond stop for coffee?

Clarissa shook her head. "I'll be fine." She leaned forward, as though angling her head three or four inches one way or the other would help her to see better. "There's movement near the house."

Toby wriggled underneath the bushes as far as he could go and sniffed. Yep. Hoomans. And vehicles. He pricked his ears. Men talking. The sound of bumps and clunks.

He scuttled backwards until close to Clarissa once more. "I can't see what's going on. I'll have to get closer."

"I don't think that's a good idea," Clarissa said automatically.

"I know *you* don't, but *I* do," Toby grumbled. "They won't see me. I'll make sure of that."

Clarissa frowned. "Alright. But be careful."

"Careful is my middle name," said Toby.

"Is it? I thought your middle name was complete-pain-in-the-derrière!"

"Funny!" Toby wagged his tail and reversed out of the hiding place. By crouching in the long grass, he could creep forward on his belly, staying well out of view. However, as he drew nearer to the house, he realised that he could probably be seen by anyone looking out of the upper windows.

If anyone was inside and staring out ... but he couldn't be sure that was the case.

Close enough, he thought, sinking onto his belly to observe the scene.

The house seemed innocuous enough, and yet it wasn't quite right. *Maybe that's my imagination*, thought Toby. *Something to do with the peeling paintwork and the dead ivy that clings to the walls and the dead rats in the outhouse and the woman with the glowing eyes ...*

But—he surveyed the grand old mansion—there *had* been a few changes.

Dating back from the eighteenth century probably, and then 'improved' during the nineteenth, it must once have been a splendid affair. Spread over three floors with a cellar below, he recalled that the rooms on the ground and first floor were spacious with high ceilings. On the top floor, the rooms were not as large, and many had damp where rain had started seeping in through the roof. It didn't surprise him at all to see that the men he'd heard conversing were construction workers. Scaffolding had been built around the far end of the house, and it looked as though they were undertaking remedial repairs to the roof and the upper floor.

In addition to that, the front door was off its hinges and a man appeared to be digging out chunks of wood from where the locks had been. Meanwhile, half a dozen glaziers were replacing numerous ground-floor windows, including the big ones on either side of the front door. Toby recalled that one of those rooms had been a library or a music room. Simply seeing the house without boarded-up windows gave Toby a start. The house appeared cleaner, more alive ...

As he observed and pondered, a van trundled along the track. It must have passed Clarissa on the way here. Toby hoped she'd remained out of sight. Toby examined the denim-blue and mustard-yellow livery on the side panel of the van. Distinctive and yet somehow still classy. *Audrey Tyler*, he read. *Interior Designer.*

Has Audrey bought this place? Or is she interior designer-ing it for someone else?

As Audrey parked up, another van arrived—this one about the size of an estate car and black with an enormous sunflower motif—and parked behind her. *Lazy Susan's Flowers*, the wording on the side read.

Toby watched, entranced. A woman in pale yellow overalls jumped out of the front seat of the new van and hurried around the back to yank open the doors. She carefully lifted out an arrangement of flowers almost as tall as her and carried it to the front door. This was the most sensational array of cut flowers Toby had ever seen. Orange and yellow blooms with a dozen deep red roses, plenty of gypsophila and sprays of red furry fern fronds to complete an autumnal look.

It's all go, thought Toby. *How much is all this costing?*

The florist didn't stay long. She hopped back in her van, performed a nippy three-point turn that Toby found admirable and scooted back down the lane. He remained where he was a while longer, watching the chaps in hard hats working on the roof and in the windows, but with no sign of anyone interesting, he realised he had two choices. He could either sneak into the house or return to Clarissa.

The chances of him entering the house with so many people around were limited, he decided. Besides which, if he did so, it was likely Clarissa would have a nervous breakdown or attempt to come in after him.

He couldn't risk putting her in danger.

He shuffled slowly backwards, anxious not to make any sudden movements that might draw attention, staring back at the house as he went. Something—a shape—materialised momentarily in a window on the left of the house on the first floor, but when Toby stared directly at it, that thing had disappeared.

His heart skipped a beat.

Something and nothing, he told himself.

But he didn't like it. Not one bit. He resumed the backwards shuffle until he felt he was clear and then lunged under the bushes and pushed his way through to Clarissa's side. She was sitting like a garden gnome, her knees to her chest, her shoulders hunched. "Thank goodness," she whispered. "I was beginning to get worried."

"Did you see the vans?" Toby whispered.

"Yes. Someone is doing the house up. Maybe the owner wants to sell it?"

"Or maybe they're moving in," said Toby. "Why would they have flowers delivered to a house that's in complete upheaval?"

Clarissa shrugged. "You'd be amazed what people do when they're trying to sell a property. They stage it. Make it look desirable."

"Oh." *Hoomans are weird*, thought Toby. *Always finding new ways to waste money.*

"I think we should go," said Clarissa. "It's getting busy."

Toby agreed. As they made their way back down the track, they caught the deep drone of yet another vehicle. It lumbered towards the gate and once more, Toby and Clarissa ducked out of sight. Toby watched as the driver leaned out and thumbed some numbers into a keypad on the gatepost. A dismembered female voice announced, "The gate is opening," and it swung wide all by itself.

"Swanky," said Clarissa.

"And brand new," said Toby.

"Someone is pouring a lot of money into all this." For the first time, Clarissa sounded suspicious. Toby wasn't sure what had changed—perhaps she simply didn't trust people with too much disposable income —but he approved of her tone.

They huddled together as this van lurched through the yawning gap and rumbled past them. It sounded heavy, the engine straining to carry the weight. "Jurassic Kitchens," Clarissa remarked. "They're putting a new kitchen in. Wow."

Definitely a hint of jealousy there, decided Toby.

"Who knew dinosaurs made kitchens?" Toby joked and streaked through the gate before it closed, leaving Clarissa to climb over by herself.

CHAPTER SEVEN

Clarissa sat at the dining table, her laptop in front of her. For once she wasn't typing, simply gazing into space, her fingers tangled together under her chin.

"Are you trying to think of a word?" Toby asked from his place on the rug where he was attempting a crossword puzzle. "Perhaps I can help." He indicated the dictionary by his side.

They'd returned from the house, wading through commuter and school-run traffic at about half eight and, after a quick breakfast, Clarissa had pressed on with some work she needed to do. Toby had idly listened to Clarissa sigh and curse and punch keys with a level of exasperation that was difficult to ignore. *It must be a tricky story she's working on*, he decided, before blocking her tetchiness out and sitting alone with his thoughts for a while, processing what he'd seen this morning.

And what had he seen?

Lots of expensive activity on a ramshackle house badly in need of restoration.

He hadn't seen The Pointy Woman. He hadn't seen any captive dogs. He hadn't seen anyone killing rats and hanging them by the tails. In fact, he hadn't seen any suspicious activity at all bar the fleeting appearance of an indistinct shape. And even that meant nothing. Not really.

But he couldn't shake his feeling of unease. *You can tart that grotty house up as much as you like, but it will still be a wolf in sheep's clothing. There's something rotten at the heart of it.*

"Mm?" Clarissa blinked and came back to the present. "Sorry? I was miles away."

"At a house in the country, by any chance?" Toby asked. "I can't get it out of my head either."

"I think I may have found something out," Clarissa said slowly. "But I don't know what it means."

Toby perked up. Crossword forgotten, he scurried over to Clarissa's side. "What? Sharesies!"

She sighed and pressed a key on her keyboard. The laptop lit up, exposing the screen she'd been reading. The text was particularly dense, with links and buttons and no pictures. It didn't look a lot of fun.

"I did a few searches to identify that house, specifically the address. It doesn't have a number—no surprise there—but it does have a name. Most recently it's been known as Hightop Hall, so I did some research into that. It turns out that prior to being renamed Hightop Hall in 1928, it was called Blackwell Manor."

"Ooh." Toby pulled a face. "That's the name we saw on the sign."

"That's right. It looks like it's going to be called by its old name. But anyway—" Clarissa waved a hand. "I went to the Land Registry website to see who owns the property and maybe find out whether it had been sold in the past few weeks. You remember Ed said that someone called Adalin Minovska owned it?"

Oh, right. Yes. That was the name. "Yes."

"Well as far as I can make out, she still does." Clarissa showed him another page. This one looked like some sort of property website. "I've tried checking all sorts of sites for recent sales in this area and I haven't come across anything for Hightop Hall."

"Suggesting that Mrs Minovska is still the owner," Toby surmised.

"It's possible that the data hasn't been updated yet," Clarissa said. "I don't imagine things happen that quickly." Clarissa clicked through to something else. "From there I decided to start digging into this Adalin Minovska, and I found out something rather baffling about her. Being a Russian émigré, we can assume she wasn't born in the UK so I won't be able to access a birth certificate. The problem is she bought the house in—" Clarissa paused for effect.

Toby huffed. "Come on!"

"In 1917."

Toby did some maths. *Nah. Does not compute.* "Huh?"

"Exactly. She presumably bought it after fleeing from Russia at the time of the revolution."

"It must have been passed to someone else in her family," Toby said. He'd known some old people in his time—Old Joe, Mrs Crouch, Old Pete, and what about Rory he'd met the previous day? Rory was old.

"That's what I thought, so I've done some cross-checking. I haven't exhausted the research yet, so yeah, I still need to do some more digging ... but for now, the most interesting thing I've found is that as I'd expect, Blackwell Manor does figure on the 1921 Census of England and Wales. What's weird, though, is that the occupants are listed as Roald Keates, a bachelor aged forty-seven born in Exeter, and our friend Adalin Minovska, a spinster aged fifty-three and born in St Petersburg, Russia." Clarissa scratched her head. "Now if she was that age in 1921, then she was born in 1868! There's no way she still owns the house."

"Not without being the oldest person on the planet," agreed Toby.

"I don't know how that helps us with our friend The Pointy Woman, but I'm intrigued now." She pulled her notebook towards her and flipped to a clean page. "I'm going to make some notes and then we'll have some lunch."

"Sounds good," said Toby. He stood and stretched. Downward dog. Upward dog. Rump on floor. Bark at the moon stretch. Nice. "I might go for a wander ..."

"Mmm?" Clarissa already had her head in whatever she was writing on her notepad.

Toby slid out into the kitchen. "Won't be long," he called, and jumped through the dog flap.

Lazy Susan's Flowers just happened to be across the road from the park. Unlike the teeny florist on Mayflower Lane—Blooming Lovely, that one was called—this one was upmarket and a tad pretentious. That's what Clarissa said anyway. It inhabited a double-fronted shop with enormous glass windows that displayed hugely complicated and over-the-top arrangements of flowers. They were undeniably lovely, and prohibitively expensive. Perfect for large houses and big weddings or funerals but far too costly for a simple bouquet for a loved one.

Toby didn't exactly know what he was hoping to achieve at the florist but nonetheless, he waited for an unsuspecting customer to push open the door and darted inside with her. Fortunately there was no-one at the counter, so he hid among the containers of gypsophila and took his bearings.

Flower shops are funny things. They smell both sweet and rancid at the same time. The scent of rotting vegetation mingled easily with the heady fragrance of freesias, stocks and lilies of the valley, so that Toby didn't know whether to gag or sneeze. He stared at the displays of roses above his head. So many varieties. Mrs Crouch loved roses, and she had half a dozen different types, but here there were roses in every colour imaginable—from white and cream to one that was so red it was almost black, and even a blue variety!

Toby—who'd studied flowers, shrubs and weeds in one of his precious books—spotted gerberas, hydrangeas, carnations in multiple hues, delphiniums and snapdragons, asters, dianthuses and larkspur. The buckets on the floor held all the fillers: ferns, ivy, eucalyptus, lemon leaf, leather leaf, myrtle and Monte Casino. There were several stands full of spools of different colour ribbons along with card spinners and decorative bits and bobs.

Classy bits and bobs, naturally. None of your cheap tat here.

A woman in peach overalls came to the counter to greet the customer. Toby studied her carefully. He couldn't be sure, but this didn't seem to be the same woman he'd seen at the house this morning.

"Good afternoon. How may I help you?" she was asking.

The customer, a stout woman wearing sensible shoes and a dogtooth coat, began talking about an event at the town hall. Toby took the opportunity to slip out of his hiding place and slink through into the back of the shop, where he again burrowed among the blooms.

Make like a flower, he told himself, channelling his inner petal and peering out between the fronds of a fern that tickled his nose.

He needn't have worried. With no-one else out here, the coast was clear.

*Why is it that it's always **behind** the actual shop where all the magick happens?* Toby wondered and pitter-pattered across the brick-red tiles, over the cut stems of a thousand flowers, towards a desk. He'd seen this in Sweet Pea's Parlour for Pampered Pooches, where the front of the shop was pretty and enticing and the rear resembled a bomb site, but the end product—fashioned inside the bomb site—was sparkly and beautiful.

The florist had left the bottom drawer of her desk open. Toby obliged by poking his nose inside. He didn't find much of interest. Lots of elastic bands and plain cards, a stapler and some sachets of strange, sticky liquid. Using the drawer as a step, he climbed onto the swivel chair and, moving carefully, balanced himself on the desktop.

Ooh! Here! Right in front of him was an enormous ledger, drawn with columns, with scribbles running down the page. *Orders*, he read on the top of the page.

Mrs Tilbury, 6 Shaldon Drive, 50-stem honeysuckle bouquet.

Nope.

Chrissie Wilde, to collect 10.30, dozen red roses.

S. *Marshall, 14 Seaview Terrace, pink spray.*

Toby read on, fascinated by the names, addresses and the variety of arrangements available, as well as the handwriting and the spelling mistakes. Nothing about Hightop Hall.

He flipped back to the previous page, and that's when he noticed the note 'autumnal table display'. Heart beating, he looked for the address. Blackwell Manor. That had been the house's original name and the one on the signpost. *Interesting!*

And who'd ordered the display?

"Hey!" The florist had appeared at the door.

Hurriedly, Toby clamped his paw on the ledger and scanned across the columns for the name. *Mme Minovska*, it said. That was it!

"What are you doing in here?" the florist asked.

"I do beg your pardon." Toby eased himself down into the chair. It started to spin. *Eurgh.* He didn't particularly want to jump off it. He was still feeling tender from the disastrous bicycle crash.

Fortunately for him, the florist caught hold of the chair and reached for his collar.

"Ah, ah, ah!" Toby warned her. "Don't touch the goods if you can't afford to pay for them." He dodged her hand and slithered to the floor.

"You can't be in here," the florist said, reaching for him again.

"I'm done, don't worry!" Toby skipped through the door separating the front from the back, bowed at the customer—who blinked at him in surprise—and positioned himself in front of the door.

"He's not yours, is he?" the florist asked the customer.

"No, no. I don't like animals." The woman pulled a face.

Toby arched an eyebrow. "Well maybe, just maybe, they don't like you either." He turned his head to gaze at the florist. "Any chance you could be a dear and open the door for me?"

"Should I let him out?" the florist puzzled. "What if he runs onto the road?"

"That's his owner's lookout, isn't it?" the customer said.

"Ooh, aren't you delightful?" Toby could hardly hide his shock.

"I suppose." The florist opened the door and Toby swaggered out, tail high.

"Bye, 'ladies'!" he called and, certain they'd be watching him, made his way down the road directly towards the crossing, where he waited patiently for the green man to appear. When it did, he sashayed across, wishing his bottom could smirk.

He hadn't been meaning to take a detour into the park. Clarissa had promised him a sammich after all —or lunch, but he hoped it would be a sammich—but the opportunity to demonstrate to the snooty old bats in the flower shop his capacity to be safe on the road had been too much to resist.

And now I'm here, I might as well make the most of it, thought Toby, and he promptly began checking his peemails.

"Well, hello again, young man!"

Toby glanced up to see Rory smiling at him. He was using a walking stick today, but he carried his shopping bag in his free hand.

"Hi, Rory!" Toby wagged his tail. It was always nice to bump into friends, old and new. "I didn't expect to see you again so soon."

"Ha." Rory cleared his throat. "Truth is, lad, I was hoping to bump into you."

"You were?" Toby pricked his ears up. *Could be interesting.*

"Come with me," Rory suggested. "Let's find a free bench."

Toby dutifully accompanied Rory on a half circuit of Swan Lake, where many of the benches were located. This was a popular place to sit and drink coffee, eat lunch or maybe daydream for a while, so there weren't many empty benches. There was space available for Rory to sit if he wanted to join someone else, but sharing didn't appear to be on the agenda. Rory wanted a bench to himself.

Toby followed, observing how the old man limped today, worried he wouldn't be able to walk far. They finally struck lucky when a woman with a pushchair vacated her seat as Toby and Rory approached.

"Ahhhh!" Rory breathed a sigh of satisfaction as he lowered himself down. "The old rheumatics are playing up a bit today."

"Sorry to hear that," Toby said politely. "Have you tried turmeric? Old Joe used to swear by it when he had aches and pains."

"Did he now?" Rory smiled. "I'm not one for spices ..."

"You can add it to soup or stew," Toby told him. "It's extremely beneficial."

"I'll keep that in mind," Rory said. "But I'm old. Old people ache. It's the natural order of things."

Toby sat down by Rory's feet and gazed at him. "Do you mind me asking how old you are?"

Rory made a soft noise in his throat. "Therein lies a story, my fine furry friend."

"I like stories!"

"Perhaps ..." Rory tipped his head back and studied the sky. Up, way above their heads, the clouds were racing, although here on the ground, only a gentle breeze ruffled Toby's fur.

Chaos above. Calm below.

"I'm not sure it's a story for today," Rory decided. "But suffice to say, I am old and then some."

Tony wondered how old that might be. Older than Old Joe had been? Older than Mrs Crouch? When you're not quite two, that's pretty old.

"I wanted to talk to you about something serious, Toby," Rory said, pulling his shopping bag onto his lap.

"I'm all ears," said Toby, wondering where that expression had suddenly come from. He evidently wasn't *all* ears because he only had two of them. Still ...

Slowly extracting his lunch box, Rory popped the lid and pulled out a neatly cut quarter-sandwich. To Toby's trained eye, it appeared to be plain cheese with butter. Nothing fancy, but still nomworthy.

Rory offered the quarter to Toby. "Would you like some?"

Argh. It broke Toby's heart to turn a sammich down, but after the adventure with the zombies, he'd promised Clarissa that he would never again accept snacks from strangers or eat rubbish he found on the street. "Thank you, but Clarissa is making me lunch at home right now," said Toby. "Your sammich looks delicious though!"

Rory nodded. He replaced the sandwich and pulled out an old-fashioned thermos flask decorated with a green and blue tartan pattern. Toby observed as Rory laboriously unscrewed the cup and set it down on the arm of the bench. He followed this with the flask lid, which he placed on top of the shopping bag, his inflamed fingers making the process impossibly slow. Finally, he poured out some hot liquid.

Toby sniffed. Tea.

Old people love tea, Toby acknowledged.

"You took me by surprise the other day when you mentioned Miranda Dervish," Rory said, his voice quiet and full of pain. "I knew her."

Toby didn't immediately process the words. "You ... Pardon me?"

"A long time ago now. But I knew your Miranda Dervish." He took a sip of his tea. "Not that that's her real name."

Toby swallowed hard. "It isn't?"

"She's been known by many names in many places."

"That sounds rather mysterious," said Toby. *And worrying.*

"She's driven by ambition and her lust for power. She's an evil creature."

That much Toby already knew. "How do you know her?" he asked, curious and yet strangely wary at the same time. The blood in his veins fizzed with anxiety, as though merely talking about The Pointy Woman might conjure her here and now right before their eyes.

Rory choked. "I can't talk about that. Not now—" His eyes lifted from Toby, staring out beyond the lake to the far side of the park. "Suffice to say, I have many, many regrets."

Puzzled, Toby remained quiet, waiting to see what else Rory would tell him.

"If I could turn back time ..." Rory shook his head. "Alas, none of us can do that."

Toby thought of Old Joe. "I wish that too."

"But ... you and I meeting? You speaking of her? That's no coincidence. The fates throw people together for a reason, and we wizards can never deny our destiny."

Toby swallowed.

"You told me that she'd killed Joseph—"

"She did."

"You also said you hadn't managed to bring her to justice. Not yet, you said."

"That's right." Toby frowned. "But I will. And soon!"

Rory lifted his cup of tea and stared into it. "You sound so certain of that," he said, and dotted his fingertip into the liquid to extract a tiny black fly. A thunderfly, Old Joe would have called it.

"I am certain, because although she fled, she's come back!"

Rory gently deposited the fly on the side of the bench and blew on it. "You're convinced of that?"

"I've seen her."

"Where?"

Was it Toby's imagination or did the breeze suddenly intensify, the promise of winter riding on its coattails, chilling his bone marrow? A hand seemed to close over his head and gently press down, mussing his fur, caressing his ears. Warm. Loving.

Shhhh, the wind whispered.

Toby shivered. He had to be hallucinating? The wind had sounded like Old Joe. Could it be a warning? He scanned the sky. The clouds were gathering, the day beginning to darken.

Rory stared at him.

"At a dog show in Birmingham," said Toby. "I'm certain it was her."

"Only there?" Rory grunted his disappointment.

Toby realised he'd have to say more. He'd already kind of inferred that she'd returned here to this Devon backwater. "I recognised her there because I thought I'd seen her at a country house on the way to Lyme. I was there looking for a friend."

"Blackwell Manor?" Rory asked.

Toby shrugged. He didn't want to give too much away. He had no idea whether Rory was trustworthy or not, but one of the first lessons he'd learned as an apprentice wizard was that he should trust his intuition. And right now, his intuition was telling him that Old Joe—or the spirit of Old Joe—had cautioned him against saying too much. Why would remain to be seen.

"I don't know the name of it," Toby said. "But it

was on a hill and had views of the sea and was surrounded by forest and fields." That pretty much described hundreds of houses on the south coast of Devon, but never mind.

"And she was living there?" Rory asked.

"I don't think she was living there. The place was a ruin. No-one could have lived there." *Apart from the Grim Brothers, maybe. But only because they were too stupid to live anywhere else. Well, serves them right. Now they reside at His Majesty's Pleasure.*

Rory leaned forward. "Toby? You haven't been back there, have you?"

Why would Rory need to know this? Toby widened his eyes. "Gosh, no. I don't have any means of transport. It's too far to walk."

Rory nodded. "And your mistress?"

Leave Clarissa out of this, mister. Toby fought to keep his hackles down. "Pfft!" He snorted. "She's far too busy with her career to chase around the country on a whim."

"Good." Rory breathed. It sounded like relief. "Toby, you need to promise me you'll keep away from Blackwell Manor."

Toby pricked his ears up. "Why?"

"Once upon a time, it was owned by ... a woman ... a notoriously bad woman."

"A witch?"

"Some say witch," Rory whispered. "Others called her a demon."

A heavy blot of water spattered on the end of Toby's nose, making him jump.

"It's raining!" Rory tipped out the remains of his tea and fastened his flask securely. "I forgot to bring a brolly." He pushed himself off the bench.

"Tell me more!" Toby said, half closing his eyes as the rain began to pummel his forehead. If Rory had more information about Miranda Dervish, he wanted to hear it.

"It'll have to wait for another time, Toby," Rory said, flipping the hood of his raincoat over his head. "But I must emphasise one thing." He began to walk to the exit, hurrying as best he could—which wasn't particularly hurriedly at all. "You *must* stay away from that house. If Miranda is there, she's undoubtedly consolidating her power."

"But—"

"She's dangerous. Incredibly dangerous. And so is that house. Stay away!"

CHAPTER EIGHT

"S'up, bro?" Sal, splayed on his back on Toby's favourite cushion, continued munching on something that might have been a cream cracker. There were several others in a pile beside him.

Toby stood at the threshold to his wizard shack, rainwater dripping from him, and gazed inside. On days like today, he wholeheartedly wished he'd been able to persuade Clarissa to install a wood burner in the corner. How cosy would that be?

"Where'd you get that cracker from?" he asked.

"Clarissa brought me a couple out. She was looking for you. I tried to tell her you weren't here, but she doesn't understand me." Sal shrugged and resumed munching.

"I think she could probably work out that I

wasn't here," said Toby. "Were those crackers for you or me?"

"Probably to share," Sal admitted.

"There's only two left."

Sal reached for another one and took a hasty bite, crumbs scattering everywhere. "One now," he said, with his mouth full.

"Were they accompanied by cheese?" Toby asked. Clarissa would never offer him plain crackers!

"I can neither confirm nor deny the previous existence of cheese," Sal declared, which Toby took to mean 'yes'.

"Good grief." Toby turned on his heel and raced for the dog flap, but when he exploded into the kitchen, he quickly realised how still and quiet the house was. "Clarissa?" he barked, skipping through into the lounge. She wasn't sitting at the table, and her bag and laptop weren't in their customary places.

She'd gone out.

Without him!

"Hmpf! The absolute cheek of it!"

But with the laptop gone, that meant she was working, not cheating on him with DC Ed.

Just as well, thought Toby. *Just as well.*

Especially for Ed.

Toby sniffed the chair and under the table. She'd

had cheese and crackers for lunch too. He climbed onto her chair to check whether she'd left any crumbs for him to snaffle. He was out of luck. She'd cleaned up. She had left him a note, however.

Dear Toby, it read, in Clarissa's familiarly hurried scrawl. *I need to check on something so I'm nipping out. I'll be back by teatime. I've left some biscuits in your bowl. Love C xxx.*

Toby jumped from the chair and raced back into the kitchen to check on his bowl. The biscuits Clarissa had left for him were of the dog variety and not chocolate or sugary, pink wafers—currently a favourite, if not a favourite favourite—as he'd hoped. *Bah!*

But thanks for the love, Clarissa. That'll fill me up.

Not.

As a mark of protest, Toby left the biscuits where they were and slunk outside into the rain. The other problem he had with Clarissa not being at home was that he had no-one to towel him off. He supposed he could visit Mrs Crouch, but she might not be best pleased, and he certainly didn't want to do anything that might alienate her and, therefore, adversely affect his supply of homemade cheesy treats!

Toby reappeared at the door of the wizard shack

and made a great show of shaking himself. Water flew in every direction. Sal wrinkled his nose and closed his eyes. Once Toby had managed to rid himself of most of the excess, he stepped inside the shack and sank into his basket. Only then did he notice that Sal was wielding a couple of Toby's colouring pencils and a length of coloured yarn.

"What are you doing?" Toby asked. The pencils, one blue and one green, were shorter than most of the others stored in the broken mug because they happened to be Toby's favourite colours and he used them the most often.

"I'm teaching myself to knit," Sal told him.

"Oh," said Toby. After a beat, he added, "Why?"

"Winter's on its way, innit?" Sal said. "I decided I fancy a hat and scarf for me good self. I used to get proper cold down that sewer."

"Uh-huh." *I can understand that.* "But you don't live in the sewer anymore."

"Thanks to you, kind sir, thanks to you. And it's much appreciated, much appreciated, I can tell ya!"

"It's no problem." Toby lay his head down, still watching Sal grapple with the yarn.

"Casting on's the difficult bit," said Sal, making a complete hash of it.

"It looks like it."

"What 'ave you been up to this morning, guv'nor?" Sal asked.

"I went to a florist—"

"Mayflower Lane?" Sal looked up. He'd managed to get the wool wrapped around his wrist but hadn't noticed.

"No, the other one, opposite the park."

"Oh yeah. I know the one you mean. The posh one."

"That's right."

"Buying flowers for Clarissa, were ya?"

"Mmm, noooooo." It had never occurred to Toby that he should. "I was having a wander—"

"Trespassing," Sal translated.

"Then I went into the park and met a wizard."

"You met a wizard?" Sal shook his head. "How does that happen? I'd never met a wizard in my life—or a witch—until I met you, but suddenly the world is full of 'em!"

Toby chuckled. But Sal had a point. *How does that happen?* Maybe, as Rory had said, the fates had brought them together. They'd brought Old Joe to him. And Clarissa. And Mrs Crouch. And—

"So what did you do with the wizard?" Sal asked, glancing at the ceiling. The rain hammered down, so loud now that they had to raise their voices. "A rain dance?"

"We chatted."

"You chatted?" Sal sounded less than impressed. "That's not a very wizardly thing to do."

Toby sat up. "Do you honestly think that when wizards get together they dance around and conjure stuff?"

"Yeah." Sal looked perturbed. "That's what I'd do with my wizard mates. If I was a wizard. Which I'm not. But if I was!"

Toby tutted. "Take it from me, that's not what we do."

"Please tell me you don't simply sit around and drink tea!" Sal was appalled by the idea.

Toby recalled Rory's tartan flask. "Mmm. Kind of."

"So disappointing," muttered Sal, dropping a coil of yarn.

"He was warning me to stay away from you-know-where."

It took Sal a moment, but he got there. "That awful house?" he whispered. "Well, he ain't wrong, is he? Ugh!" He shivered. "I don't ever wanna go back there!"

"But I do!" said Toby. "And the more I think about our conversation, the more I want to."

Sal cocked his head. "You're a contrary canine, ain't ya?"

"It isn't that. The discussion I had with Rory—that's his name—wasn't properly concluded. There was a lot he didn't say. He claims to have known The Pointy Woman. He knows about the house. He was warning me off, and yet he wouldn't tell me anything about how he knows her. Or knew her. Or whatever. Don't you find that odd?"

Sal regarded Toby in confusion, dropping another coil of yarn. "Ya know, I don't wanna be *that* rat, but erm, he genuinely may fear for your safety. Telling you to avoid a woman who kills people for fun *and* stay away from a house where they happily hang rats by their tails for decoration, ya know what that sounds like to me? That sounds like the *sanest* thing I've ever 'eard, mate!"

"No need to get aerated," said Toby. "You may be right, but you weren't there, and I'm going off what my gut told me."

Sal squinted at him. "Were your guts empty, perchance?"

Toby pulled a face. "They were, as a matter of fact."

"Nuff said, me old pal. Nuff said." Sal nodded with satisfaction and tugged at the loose wool, tightening it around his back leg. "What's goin' on 'ere with this bloomin' yarn?"

"I want to go back." Toby was nothing if not stubborn. "But I don't want to involve Clarissa."

"You're not going to try cycling again, are ya?" Sal asked, frowning as he tugged on the wool, trying to free it. The more he pulled, the tighter it became, his hind leg hoisted into the air, his front paw unable to straighten.

"Clarissa took the bicycle back to Mason's house, so unless I nick it off him again, that'll be a no." Toby sighed and tipped his head back, staring at the mobile that dangled from the ceiling. The planets danced around the sun. "I wish I had a spaceship—"

"You don't wanna be travelling short distances in a spaceship," said Sal, who was a bit of a science-fiction fan on the sly. "They go too fast for short distances. You need a helichopper."

"Oh, that would be good!" Toby enthused. Every time he heard a helicopter, he'd dash up onto the roof of the wizard shack and watch it, wagging his tail in case the pilot was looking down on him. "Bit noisy though. If *she* was there, she'd hear me coming a mile off."

"True, true. Something quieter would be better." Sal grimaced as the wool—wrapped tightly around his leg—began to cut the circulation off.

"A magick carpet!" said Toby, taking a renewed interest in the old rug Clarissa had given him to cover the linoleum on the shed floor. As you can imagine, it could get cold under his tootsies so she'd bought one in a charity shop. He considered how difficult it might be to conjure a spell to turn the tootsie-warming floor covering into a magnificent flying machine.

"Or a hot air balloon," said Sal.

"That would be cool, too," Toby agreed, scuffing the edge of the rug to take a better look at the underside. A tad threadbare, but what if—

"I know someone with a hot air balloon."

Toby stopped scuffing the rug and stared at Sal. "What?"

"I know someone with a hot air balloon." Sal tugged hard at the wool wrapped around his wrist and leg and finally unbalanced altogether. "Timber!" he yelled, and promptly toppled over. Fortunately, the cushion ensured he had a soft landing. "Eeek! Help me!"

Toby rolled his eyes but managed to drag himself out of his basket and help Sal untangle himself. In the end, he had to nibble through the wool so the rat could free his back leg. "Uuuuh! My leg's gone to sleep!" Sal complained, hopping around.

"It's a good job you have three others!" said Toby.

Sal pouted. "No need to be mean. Weren't I sympa-fetic when you crash-landed the other day?"

"You have four legs, I only have one tongue," Toby pointed out.

"Even so!" Sal rubbed the feeling back into his leg.

Certain the rat would live to faint another day, Toby returned to his basket, kicking down the edge of the rug as he passed. "What were you saying about a friend with a hot air balloon?" he asked.

"To be fair, he's not a friend."

"Okay?"

"In fact, I've never even met 'im, but I 'ave *'eard* of 'im!" He drew the word heard out as though to emphasise that he did exist.

"Oh." This sounded less hopeful to Toby. He began to reconsider the rug.

"While I was visiting West Hill way with Pom and his family, they was talking about this enterprising chap in the woods nearby who'd started this hot air balloon hire business."

"A hot air business in the woods?" Toby was flummoxed. How did you fly a hot air balloon out of a wooded area? Didn't you need a lot of space to do that?

"Yeah, yeah." Sal warmed to his theme. "It was such a new business it had yet to take off."

There was silence.

Sal regarded Toby. Toby regarded Sal.

"Boom boom?" tried Sal, and fell about laughing.

"Good grief." Toby lay his head down in his basket and buried his eyes under his paws. "You had me going for a minute. I actually believed you!"

"Heeheeheeheeheeheeheehee!"

Toby uncovered one eye and watched the fat rat writhe with mirth. *Hooligan*!

"Heeheeheeheeheeheeheehee!"

Toby chuckled. Sal's laugh was infectious. "Behave!"

"Hahaha! Heehee! Thing is ... heeheeheehee! I did actually heehee-hear about a hahaha-hot air business."

"Whereabouts in the woods?"

Sal waved a vague paw to his right. "Somewhere."

"That's not helpful, Sal!"

"I don't have a map!" protested Sal. "I told you, I never saw it, I only *heard* of it!"

"Hmm. Well, in that case, you can help me find it."

"You wha'?"

"We'll go and look for it together."

"I'm not sure I wanna do that." Poor Sal had been suffering with a touch of agoraphobia—or cowarditis or something—since their last adventure. He feared going out in case the Mayflower Lane Mafia came after him.

"You'll be fine, I promise," said Toby. "Strength in numbers and all that. No-one will be looking for you in the woods." He jerked his head towards the door.

"You mean now?" Sal squeaked, hugging his pencil knitting needles to his chest.

"No time like the present."

"It's *raining*!"

Toby peered out of the door. The rain lashed down so hard, it bounced back off the patio and into the air. It didn't look like it was going to stop anytime soon.

"It's alright for you." Sal came to stand alongside him. There were puddles in the lawn. "You're tall. I'm not. I'll drown."

This was patently untrue. Toby was shorter than both Pickle and Pippin and not much bigger than Moriarty. But he supposed that, in comparison to Sal, he was a veritable giraffe.

"You have a point," Toby admitted. "We'll go first thing in the morning."

CHAPTER NINE

Clarissa arrived home sometime after half past five, her backpack on her back and clutching a tote bag half-full of shopping and her umbrella. "Ugh! I'm drenched!" she complained, throwing the brolly in the sink and dropping the groceries on the counter before chucking her sopping backpack under the dining table in the living room. "Who ordered this weather?"

"Not me," said Toby, catapulting himself through his dog flap to greet her before belatedly remembering he was in a huff because he hadn't had cheese and crackers for lunch.

"How are you doing, furry boy?" Clarissa bent down and kissed his head.

"All the better for seeing you!" That much was

true. Clarissa had the capacity to instantly illuminate his world, much as Old Joe once had. "What's for dinner?" he asked, one eye on the bag with the groceries.

"Cupboard love. That's all you have for me," Clarissa complained. "I thought I'd do something with pasta. It's been a while."

"Ooh." Toby's ears pricked up.

"A bit of spag bol? Whaddayareckon?" Clarissa grinned and tipped out the bag's contents. Mince. An onion. Dried pasta. Mushrooms. Some green stuff ...

"Sounds good to me."

Clarissa pulled the big frying pan out of the cupboard and set it on the hob. After setting its bottom on fire—*whoosh*—she reached for the oil. "Where did you get to earlier? You told me you were nipping out."

"I did nip out. But it wasn't as nippy as I'd planned," said Toby, watching her rummage in the utensil drawer for her sharpest knife. "I visited Lazy Susan's Flowers."

"You did?" Clarissa held the onion down and sliced and diced it.

"I did," Toby replied, nodding once, a single, grand gesture. *Behold my brilliance!*

"And what did she have to say for herself?" She threw the onion into the pan, where it began to sizzle, and reached for the garlic.

Toby had a feeling Clarissa wasn't taking him entirely seriously. "We didn't converse, obvs!"

Clarissa giggled as the garlic met a similar fate to the onion. "Tell me what you found out, o' pompous one."

Hmpf. "The flowers we witnessed being delivered this morning were ordered by none other than Mum-me Minovska."

Clarissa half turned. "Mummy?"

"That's what it said in the book," Toby explained. "I imagine it's some sort of Eastern European forename."

"Spell it?"

"M-m-e."

Clarissa tittered and turned her attention to the garlic once more. "I think you probably mean Madame."

"Oh." Toby was none the wiser.

"Funnily enough, I've been trying to track that particular lady down all afternoon, too. I went to visit my old friends at the *Sun Valley Tribune* and while I was there had a dig through the archive. I did find a few images of Hightop Hall—or Blackwell Manor—

over the ages, but our Madame Minovska is an extremely elusive lady. However—Ooh! One sec—" Clarissa crumbled the mince into the pan and began stabbing it with her big silicon spoon. "Just let me get this cooking ..."

Toby lifted his nose and indulged in a sniff. *Mmm. Why do frying onions smell so good when they are so bad for me? Totally* unfair!

Once Clarissa was satisfied everything was under control, she washed her hands and moved into the living room to begin rooting through her backpack. After unzipping the main compartment and removing her laptop, scattering its cables, her notebook, ear pods, her purse, a bruised apple, some tissues, a couple of bills and a half-empty bottle of water all over the floor, she *actually* located what she was looking for in the *front* pocket. She produced a battered old book with a flourish. "Ta-dah! I put it in there to keep it safe."

"It looks old," said Toby. It smelt old too. Musty and dusty.

"I went to the library on my way home and had a quick look in the local history section. They have books going way back to the nineteenth century, but most of them are for reference only."

Toby's ears pricked at this. How wonderful it

would be to sit in a library for a few hours and read ancient magick books. He wondered whether that would be possible. "What's this one about?" he asked.

"It's called *Peculiar Tales from Sunshine Valley and Surrounds* by F.J. Emmett, a good local name if ever I heard one."

"Effjay is a local name?"

"No. Emmett is." Clarissa rolled her eyes. "I was drawn to this one because he—I'm assuming F.J. was male, but you never know—says in the introduction that the tales in the book are merely rumours and stories passed down by locals over the years. There are all sorts of things in here, including"—Clarissa performed a sitting-down jig with her shoulders—"a story about a tree in the Blackdown Hills that had magickal powers! I had a quick look at that one, and it's a bit hit and miss—but the rumour that it existed must have been conveyed down the ages!"

"It's a good job no-one knows for sure that it does exist," said Toby, concerned for the welfare of Grappletwigs and her squirrel tribe.

"Agreed." Clarissa, remembering her frying mince, darted into the kitchen. Book in one hand and spoon in the other, she hurriedly stirred the contents of the pan.

Toby followed her through. *Can you stay in one place? I'm getting dizzy*, he thought.

"But the main reason I think this book is of interest is because it has a section on Blackwell Manor."

Toby wagged his tail. "What does it say?"

"Let me get the tomatoes in here ... hang on."

Sighing, Toby lay down on the floor and stifled a yawn. It had been a long day. He was tired. He was hungry. Still, he wanted to know what Effjay Emmett had to say about the manor.

Finally, Clarissa was happy with her concoction and the kitchen smelled of freshly chopped herbs as well as tomatoes and onions. She turned down the heat, grabbed the book and hustled Toby through into the lounge, where they cuddled together on the sofa.

"Emmett claims that there's a record of a dwelling in the Domesday Book and that originally some baron or other lived there, but that building was burned, and the land returned to the crown until sometime in the fifteenth century when it was passed to the Druett family—of Norman origin, apparently —in return for some favour or other ... to one of the kings. Can't remember. Might have been a Henry."

"That's all a bit vague," grumbled Toby.

"I'm summarising what he says." Clarissa flicked through the pages. "I think it was a Henry because there were quite a few of those around that time. Don't worry. It's not the most pertinent thing. That comes next."

"Okay. I'm listening." Toby's tummy rumbled.

"I guess the Druetts lived at the manor happily enough for a while—a couple of hundred years—and then for some reason, the locals started getting a bit twitchy about the surname."

"Druett?"

"Yes. Emmett's theory is that at the time of the persecutions for witchcraft, anyone was fair game—especially women who were different in some way, kind of out of the ordinary. A widow named Elsbeth Druett Amery was tried at Exeter Assizes for witchcraft and found guilty. She burned at the stake."

"Ugh!" Toby shuddered.

"Emmett reckons something as simple as the surname Druett sounding like 'druid' may have set some of the religious nutcases off."

"But that ... that's appalling!"

"That's history for you," said Clarissa. "Blackwell Manor was burned to the ground, or most of it, but the land remained in the Druett family—then, in the late seventeenth century, a John Matthew

Drewitt began restoring what was left of the property. The manor was extended in the eighteenth century and again in the latter half of the nineteenth century. Most of the grounds were sold off to a neighbouring farm over the years, but the house remains."

"I'm not sure how this helps us," said Toby.

"That's only the factual bit. The stuff that Emmett could prove from property records and assizes records from the archives. It's the *rumours* that are the interesting part."

"Alright."

"Starting with the one that Elsbeth Druett Amery was a witch. That she had caused her neighbouring farmer's cows to die and that was why the court handed over her land to the farmer as recompense!"

"We're not going to fall for that nonsense, are we?" Toby pulled a face. "The cows probably died because the farmer was rubbish at his job."

"Maybe, maybe." Clarissa couldn't disagree. She was well aware of the unjust persecution of women in sixteenth- and seventeenth-century Britain and beyond. "But she was disliked locally, and it was said that if she visited Sun Valley on market day, all the milk would turn sour."

Toby checked whether Clarissa was being serious before guffawing.

"Oh ye of little faith," Clarissa said, smiling. "But I have more."

Toby snuggled down. This was better than a bedtime story. He wondered whether he could borrow the book and read it to the geese in the park. Would they enjoy it as much?

"Coupled with that, there were rumours that the water in the well at the manor was black and that it had caused an outbreak of plague in the nearby villages, and that's how it became known as Blackwell Manor. When the manor was first rebuilt, several of the construction workers were killed in a freak accident when a wall collapsed. Then another one fell down the well and drowned. The site started to get a reputation for being haunted."

"Oo-er," said Toby.

"That seems to have suited John Matthew Drewitt very much because he didn't want to be bothered. He was described as an eccentric recluse who didn't pay his bills. There were lots of complaints about him and again, Emmett found references to him in court records when he was summonsed for non-payment."

"Did they burn *him* at the stake?" asked Toby. "I bet they didn't."

"I think we'd all moved on from killing witches by that time," said Clarissa. "Nothing is said about what happened to him, however—"

"Ah, yes?"

"A couple of generations on, well into the eighteenth century by now, there were more rumours of witchcraft. You'll have to read it!" She waved the book at Toby. "It's fascinating. There are descriptions of housemaids and cooks and people going missing. There was talk of a rat infestation. People spoke of parties where everyone danced naked. There's a rumour about a mass poisoning."

"Grim," said Toby. "I can't understand why anyone would persist in living there."

"That's right. We know that the house fell into disuse until it was eventually bought by the Russian émigré, right? She began its restoration."

"Yes."

"Well, when Emmett wrote and published this book in 1932 Madame Minovska was alive and still resident. She had changed the name from Blackwell Manor to Hightop Hall, probably in an effort to sanitise its reputation. Emmett describes how the house had fallen into disrepair and how she used to shuffle around the grounds wearing her widow's weeds—"

"Her what?" Toby conjured an image of a woman draped in bramble and ivy and dried grass, floating around Hightop Hall weeping into an over-size black-edged handkerchief.

"That's what they call those old black clothes that widows used to wear. There was a time when widows would wear black for the rest of their lives."

"That's sad," said Toby.

"He claims she would hold seances in the parlour, and those who attended were scared to death by what they saw and heard—"

Yoikes! "Scared to *death*?"

"Not literally," Clarissa clarified, flipping a couple of pages. "I don't think so, anyway, although that wouldn't surprise me."

"Nor me," said Toby, remembering the house and its *presence*. If he'd known any of this in advance, he would probably never have stepped inside.

Nah. He still would have done.

"Emmett also notes that Madame Minovska liked to entertain gentlemen."

"Did she sing and play the piano?" Toby asked, remembering the music room.

"I don't think Emmett means that kind of entertaining," Clarissa replied, smiling.

Toby was none the wiser.

"It was frowned upon, of course."

"You entertain Ed," Toby pointed out. "He's always over here listening to our music and watching our movies—"

"Different times," said Clarissa, moving quickly on. "But what I think Emmett is getting at is that Madame Minovska had groups of men, or several men, coming to the house. He says—" Clarissa ran her finger down the page until she found what she was looking for. "Here. Carriages were known to arrive at Blackwell Manor after dark and men in cloaks would alight there. Lights could be seen for several hours until the place was plunged into darkness as dawn approached. Then the horses would return and the cloaked visitors would depart."

"Hmmm. So she liked parties—"

"Maybe. This was five years after the First World War, so she wouldn't have been young." Clarissa shrugged. "Emmett imagines something perverse was happening inside the house, but he has no evidence of this. I think his contemporaries jumped to the wrong conclusion. I don't think she was 'entertaining' groups of men. I think she was holding gatherings for her coven. Men and women. It's difficult to tell when everyone is wearing a cloak."

"You definitely think she was a witch, then?" Toby asked.

"We can't know for sure, can we? It sounds reasonable though." Clarissa closed the book. "Read the chapter. It's interesting."

"It's unfortunate the book doesn't come right up to date," said Toby, levitating the tome out of Clarissa's hand and over to his basket to read later. "It would be good to know what happened after Madame Minovska passed away and what her link to The Pointy Woman is."

Clarissa stood and stretched. "*If* there's a link."

"Oh, there's a link," said Toby. *I know there is.*

CHAPTER TEN

Up with the dawn, Toby had rushed out to the shack to wake Sal.

The poor rat, who'd spent half the night trying to master the art of casting on, was not amused to wake and find Toby poking his belly with a colouring pencil knitting needle. "What's your game, then?" he demanded, brushing the pencil away.

"We're going in search of your balloon pal, remember."

"He's not my pal." Sal grunted, closing his eyes. "In fact, I don't even know him. Remember?"

"You know him better than I do."

"Eurgh." Sal rolled over and pulled the tea towel he used as a bedspread towards his neck. "Is it still raining?"

"No. It's the perfect day for a balloon flight," Toby told him, who had no idea whether balloons could fly in adverse conditions or not but assumed they couldn't. "So shift your furry butt."

"What about breakfast?"

Hmmm. Good point. In his excitement, Toby had almost forgotten. Clarissa wasn't yet awake, so his normal breakfast wasn't on offer. That left Mrs Crouch's treats. He levitated the Quality Street tub from its high shelf and gently brought it down onto the rug.

Sal snapped properly awake and clasped his paws together. "Cor! A breakfast for kings."

Toby opened the lid. There were seven treats inside.

"Three and a half each," said Sal.

"On your bike," said Toby and offered him two.

"Five-two is hardly fair!" Sal protested.

"Look at the size of you compared to me!" Toby pointed out. "I'm more than five times your size."

"Yeah, but you're fully grown and I'm a growing boy."

Toby had no idea how old Sal was, but he doubted he was a boy. "The only thing about you that's growing is your waistline," said Toby.

"Rude." Sal pouted.

Toby tsked but handed over another treat. This satisfied Sal, who beamed at Toby and began nibbling.

Toby ate his four treats in two bites, then stared at the empty tin regretfully. "I'll leave it down here and that way, if Mrs Crouch pops around, she'll realise that I've run out," said Toby, ever helpful.

And hopeful.

"Let's go," he said.

Sal hastily stuffed his remaining treat into his gob and hurried after Toby. They made their way to the loose fence panel at the rear of the house and through to the garden behind them. With the elderly owners still snug in bed, there were no obstacles to worry about. Following the road around, they eventually came to a piece of scrubland where the local kids liked to play ball games. In turn, this opened out into the woods, sporadically populated by young trees at first, becoming denser the deeper you went.

"Wait for me," Sal huffed. He could move quickly when he wanted to, but this morning, his motivation had yet to wake up.

Toby paused to allow Sal a chance to catch up, taking the opportunity to have a good sniff. He could smell some interesting scents. The woods always excited him. "Which way?" he asked Sal, who doubled over to catch his breath.

"I don't know!" Sal said, and coughed up a lung.

"You need to quit smoking," Toby joked. "We'll keep going towards West Hill. If you recognise anything we can stop and investigate."

"Oh, man," Sal grumbled. "Any chance of a lift?"

"Already?" Toby couldn't believe it. "You need to knit less and get out and about more!" He hunkered down, allowing Sal to grab a hold of his collar and climb onto his back.

"I'm a home-lovin' boy," said Sal. "*Rattus norvegicus* and *homus domesticas*."

"You made that up," said Toby.

"I didn't fib about being domesticated," said Sal, and dug his back heels into Toby's neck.

"Do that again and you'll be walking," said Toby. Sal sat back and behaved.

For a while, anyway.

After a couple of minutes he became bored, so he started to sing *Wand'rin' Star*. He had a voice not unlike Lee Marvin's, and so the song rather suited him. But after three renditions of the opening verse—he evidently didn't know the rest—Toby almost threw him off.

"Please stop singing," Toby pleaded.

"You know what your problem is?" Sal asked, not waiting for an answer. "You don't appreciate art when you hear it."

"That wasn't art—it sounded like someone strangling a bull," Toby rebutted.

"Cheek! I used to be a member of the choir when I was down the sewer!"

"If you'll beg my pardon, that's where *that* noise should have stayed," said Toby.

"How curious." A soft voice floated out of the nearby undergrowth, startling both Toby and Sal.

"Who's there?" Sal cried, gripping Toby's left ear with both front paws, the claws digging deep.

"Ow!" Toby complained.

"Who is it? Who is it?" hissed Sal.

"I do beg your pardon." A snowy snout pushed out of the foliage, followed by an orange head. That was enough for Sal. Letting go of Toby, he keeled over in a dead faint and slipped off his back, landing on the soft earth.

Toby wasn't sure where to look first. The fox continued to advance, while Sal lay on his back with all four paws relaxed against his undercarriage and his pink tongue poking out one side of his mouth.

In the interests of protecting his friend, Toby

stepped over Sal and moved into the fox's path. "Hey there!" he said.

"Hel-lo," replied the fox, dragging its eyes from Sal to Toby and sizing him up.

In an effort to swell his chest and make himself look larger than he was, Toby took a deep breath and rolled his shoulders back.

"I'm Toby," he said.

The fox studied him from head to toe before answering. "Frank," he said.

"How are you doing, Frank?"

"I'm very well. Thank you." Frank's eyes drifted down to Sal once more. "Is this your snack?" he asked.

"Snack?" Toby laughed nervously. "I'm afraid to say he's not a snack, he's Sal."

"A Sal snack," suggested Frank and licked his lips.

Toby shook his head. "Definitely not for eating."

"Oh, that's disappointing." Frank's orange eyes gleamed.

"I'm sorry about that. He's my friend."

"He's a rat."

"Hahaha. Well spotted. But I'm afraid this rat and I are good mates." Toby enunciated his words clearly, hoping and praying that Frank wouldn't take offence and turn on him. Foxes could be vicious, and Toby knew he'd be no match for him. The chances were both Toby and Sal would end up as Frank's TV dinner.

"That's sad," said Frank.

"Not for Sal."

Frank wrinkled his nose. "I see."

Why on earth didn't I think to bring some treats with me? wondered Toby. *It would have made sense for moments like this. I could have bribed old Frankie here with a cheesy treat and we'd have been on our way!* "I don't believe we've met before? I have met a few of your ... erm ... lookalikeys hereabouts."

Frank huffed. "I bet you've met Gormless Graham, haven't you? And Moany Mavis? They're always out and about. Not a bean of common sense between them."

Toby hadn't realised that common sense was measured in beans, but you learn something new every day.

"Lovely folk though," Toby said. "They've been teaching me about the woods and the plants and the insects. I'm looking forward to monitoring the change of seasons and learning more."

"Oh." Frank appraised Toby anew. "Un-ex-pected," he said, pronouncing every syllable discretely. "You're a fan of the countryside, I take it."

"I am. But more than that, I like learning new things." Toby prodded Sal with his paw. Sal opened one eye.

"If you want to know more, you should come to the oracle," Frank said. If he'd had long hair, he would probably have tossed it over a shoulder.

Sal, hearing Frank's voice, clamped his eye shut again. Toby poked him, harder this time.

"Who would that be?" Toby asked, not thinking.

"Me, of course." The fox's tone dripped ice.

Oopsie. Toby, realising he'd set back relations to the Cold War period, hurried to make recompense. "Of course it is! Wow! I am so happy to meet an ... an *oracle*!" He kicked Sal so that the rat had no choice but to grunt, grumble and roll over onto his belly. "You must be extraordinarily wise!"

"It has been said." Frank preened.

"Beauty *and* brains!" Toby laid it on thick.

"Oh, thank you." Frank averted his eyes, suddenly bashful, giving Toby a glimpse of a fox who acted more confident than he probably was.

He pressed home his advantage. "Sal and I are honoured to meet you, aren't we, Sal?" Toby dug a claw into Sal's backside.

Sal, cowering beneath Toby's undercarriage, squeaked.

"Honoured and humbled," Toby told Frank before dropping his head to Sal. "Climb aboard, mate. We'd best be going."

Frank watched Sal grab Toby's collar and hoist himself onto his back. And this time he managed not to salivate.

"It's nice to have met you," said Toby and, nodding, turned away in the direction of the track they'd been following before bumping into the fox.

"Are you leaving so soon?" Frank sounded crest-fallen. And strangely young.

Toby wondered how old he was.

"We're on a mission to find someone," Toby explained, glancing back over his shoulder.

"You won't know them," Sal said, and squeezed Toby's flanks with his back legs. "Onwards, fine steed."

Frank took a step after them. "I might do."

"You won't," said Sal.

Toby arched an eyebrow. "He might do," he said.

"Man-o-man-o-man-o-man. Or he might *eat* me!" Sal complained.

Toby ignored him. "We're looking for some chap that runs a hot air balloon business."

Frank thought for a moment. "A chap, you say?"

"Yes. We'd heard there was someone in the woods here—"

Frank shrugged. "I don't think so ..."

"See!" said Sal. "He knows nothing. Let's go!"

"I don't know a chap," Frank repeated, "but I do know a lady."

"A lady?" Toby tried to get a look at Sal but his head wouldn't rotate far enough.

"Hey!" Sal held his paws up. "Don't blame me, a'right? I keep tellin' ya I've never met no hot air balloon person."

"So, it's a *person* now?" Toby asked. "I swear you said 'he'."

"Person. Animal. He. She. What difference does it make?" Sal ranted. "I've never met them. I don't even know whether the geezer or geezeress exists for certain, I'm just tellin' ya what I've heard!"

"She exists," said Frank, calmly.

Toby brightened at this news. Okay, a couple of crossed wires, but they were finally on to something. "Is she a uh ... is she a vixen?" Toby asked.

"A sow," said Frank.

Oh. A pig in the forest. That was a new one on Toby, but he wasn't about to begin discriminating. If pigs wanted to live in the forest and llamas and ostriches wanted to live on farms, who was he to tell anyone they couldn't or shouldn't? To each their own.

"Is there any chance you could take us to her, please?" Toby asked.

"Or ..." Sal shrugged. "Just point the way?"

Frank beamed. "I'd be happy to take you!"

"He wants to eat me," Sal muttered. "He's looking hungrier by the minute. I bet he hasn't had any breakfast."

"Sssh!" Toby hissed at him.

"I want to liiiiiive!" Sal wailed.

Toby closed his eyes for a moment. Perhaps it would have been easier to leave Sal at home. The rat wasn't much cut out for adventures. When Toby opened his eyes again, he gazed beseechingly at Frank. "Do you solemnly swear not to eat Sal?" he asked.

Frank gave the matter careful consideration. "I will. But in exchange, would you do something for me?"

"He wants my leg," said Sal. "A morsel. A snackette."

"Pipe down!" Toby was at his wit's end. "What would you like us to do?"

Frank lay down on his belly beside Toby and

cocked his head to one side. One of his ears flopped the wrong way. Toby rather liked this. He was prone to ear malfunctions too. "Would you be my friends?" the fox asked.

Sal and Toby were surprised into silence. They regarded the fox with a mix of astonishment and delight—on Toby's part—and confusion and horror on Sal's.

"Please?"

"No," said Sal.

"Of course!" said Toby. "You can never have too many friends."

"It could all be a ruse," Sal suggested.

"I don't have any friends," Frank admitted. "The older foxes can be a bit stand-offish and territorial, and almost everyone else in the woods is afraid of me."

"You *are* a bit scary," Toby told him. "Too intense, perhaps."

"Do you think?" Frank nodded, his face serious. "I'll work on that."

"And maybe not threaten to eat folk!" Sal waved his clenched fist in Frank's direction.

"I was peckish," Frank admitted.

"We'll bring snacks when we visit again," Toby promised.

"We're coming again?" Sal sounded horrified.

"Of course!" said Toby. "You have to keep in touch with your friends! Otherwise what's the point of having them?"

Frank grinned from ear to ear. "I'm so chuffed! Thank you!"

Toby smiled. "Our pleasure. So ... er ... the hot air lady?" He didn't want to waste any more of the morning. At this rate it would be lunchtime and Frank might change his tune about Sal.

"This way!" Frank skipped off, taking them further into the woods and along the track towards West Hill. "Not far!"

And he whistled as he went.

CHAPTER ELEVEN

"Sow by Sow-west." Toby read the crooked wooden sign that had been hung on a tree with a rusty old nail. "Balloon and pilot hire."

"Cool name, isn't it?" Frank said, his eyes shining with pride. "I helped Hedda think of that."

"Hedda being ... the pig?" Toby asked.

Frank looked blank. "Pig?"

"Didn't you say she was a pig?"

"I said she was a sow," Frank said. "You asked me if she was a vixen. I don't know any pigs. I especially don't know any pigs who run hot air balloon businesses."

"Uh-huh." Toby followed Frank as he trotted through to a pretty clearing where the blustery breeze made the grass and the late summer flowers ebb and flow in waves. A heap of silky fabric in vibrant shades of pink and purple had been pegged out in the grass, and a sizable wicker shopping basket was upended beside it.

"Hedda?" Frank called. "I have some customers for you."

"*Potential* customers," said Sal.

"One second!" came a soft voice, buried somewhere near a hollowed-out log. "I'm looking for my repair kit!"

Repair kit? Toby baulked at this.

A few moments later, a sweet, brown face with black eyes, shining with intelligence, poked out of the log. "Hey, Frank! Good to see you!" Heaving herself out of the log, Hedda scuttled over to smile at Toby and Sal.

Toby gawped at her in shock. Frank was right. She wasn't a pig. She was a hedgehog!

"Who are your friends?" she asked.

Frank nodded in satisfaction at the term 'friends'. "This is Toby and his mate, Sal."

Sal slid from Toby's back and hurried forward to offer a deep bow. "Salvatore Messio," he said. "At your service, ma'am."

Toby performed a comical double take. He'd never known Sal to be so effusive, so ... so *sal*acious!

Hedda merely giggled, the prickles on her back rippling. "Pleased to meet you, Mr Messio."

Sal preened. "You *must* call me Sal."

"Sal." Hedda's warmth was intoxicating. "How may I help you boys?" she asked.

"We were hoping to hitch a ride," Toby replied, studying the silk fabric uncertainly.

"Ah." Hedda wrinkled her dainty nose. "Won't be today, I'm afraid. I've sprung a puncture."

"Awww." Toby groaned in disappointment. *Look on the bright side, though,* he told himself. *At least we know where to come now. If we decide to come back.*

It was a big 'if'.

"Anything we can help with?" Sal asked.

Toby raised an eyebrow.

"I pricked through the skin of the balloon," Hedda explained, shaking her spines. "It's an occupational hazard. I have a repair kit but the glue needs time to go hard, so it'll be tomorrow lunchtime before I can set off."

"If you need help ... blowing up the balloon, or ... pressing down on anything," Sal said, "I'm your rat."

"That's so sweet of you!" Hedda enthused. "Say, would you guys like some tea? I've brewed a batch of blackberries."

"Sounds sensational," exclaimed Sal before anyone else could answer.

"Thank you," said Toby. "I am thirsty, now you come to mention it."

Hedda nodded and disappeared into her log. Toby and Frank stood around while Sal inspected the basket and the silk balloon. "Fascinating," he kept saying.

Hedda returned with a tray of tea things, with almost the tiniest cups Toby had ever seen. In retrospect, he decided drinking out of acorns courtesy of Grappletwigs took that prize, but the blackberry tea itself was exquisite. Clarissa would have loved it.

"How've you been doing, Frank?" Hedda asked. "It's been a few weeks since you lost Fred. Feeling any better?"

Toby's head swivelled from Hedda to Frank. The fox's eyes had instantly misted up. He nodded. "I'm okay." It was a lie. Toby could see it in his face.

"Fred?" he asked.

"My brother," said Frank. "My twin. He … passed away."

"Oh, I'm so sorry for your loss," said Toby, aghast, feeling like he'd trespassed into Frank's grief. He glanced at Hedda for support.

"Snare," she mouthed, and Toby's heart sank

even further.

"You do have to be careful roaming around these woods," Frank said, and sniffed.

Sal reached out and stroked the fox's leg. "Sorry, dude," he said. "If you ever need to talk ..."

Toby could hardly believe what he was seeing. Sal making nice with a fox?

"I appreciate it," Frank replied, his voice husky. He looked away and cleared his throat.

Well, no wonder he's in need of a few friends, thought Toby.

"How many riders?" Hedda asked, changing the subject and bringing Toby back to the present.

"Pardon?" He wasn't quite with it.

"I need to know how many people I'm going to be carrying because I have to work out ballast."

"Oh, I see." Toby peered at Sal. His teeny friend didn't need to come. "Just me, I gue—"

"And me," said Sal, nodding enthusiastically at Hedda. "I'd love to go."

Hedda looked expectantly at Frank.

"I'm not invited," he said. "I—"

"Hey! The more the merrier," said Sal.

"Is now a good time to mention that this isn't a jaunt?" asked Toby. "This is deadly serious business."

"Deadly?" Hedda repeated. "What do you mean? How deadly is deadly? Because, you know, I'm not sure I'm signing up to *deadly*!"

"Don't you worry, babe!" Sal chipped in before Toby could say anything. "We won't let anything untoward happen to you!"

"My hero," said Hedda, but Toby wasn't sure she meant it. Sal didn't seem to mind though.

"I ought to explain," said Toby. "In the interests of transparency and all. You see, the thing is ... I'm seeking evidence of someone's whereabouts. Someone who did a very bad thing."

"How bad?" asked Frank, bleakly.

"Murder-y bad," admitted Toby.

Hedda caught her breath.

"This person, a woman actually—I call her The Pointy Woman but her real name is Miranda Dervish—killed my hooman, Old Joe." He hated saying her name out loud, especially in the same breath as dear Old Joe's.

"Do you think she'll kill again?" Frank asked.

"She's bound to. She's bad through and through. She has to be found."

"And then what?" Hedda asked.

Toby stared at her in surprise. This was a question no-one had ever asked him.

"Are you going to kill her?" Hedda asked, her gaze level.

These thoughts had terrorised Toby on many a night. He would lie on Old Joe's bed, unable to find a comfortable spot, worrying about what he would do when the time came to confront *her*. Sometimes he imagined he would kill her on the spot with the aid of a spell he'd discovered on the dark web. Other times, he knew he'd never be able to stomach killing her in cold blood.

But what would the alternative be?

"I don't know," he answered truthfully. "My priority is finding out, without a doubt, that she's living where I think she is."

"Alright," said Hedda. "So it'll be the four of us."

"You know, Frank, you don't have to come along if you don't want to," Toby told the fox. "We can do something together another day. Something a bit more fun. I don't want to place you on the spot—or put you in danger—when I don't know what the outcome might be."

Frank lifted his nose. "Peace," he said. "We're friends. Friends support each other."

"Great," said Hedda. "I'll get on with fixing the balloon and I'll see you all tomorrow after lunch!"

CHAPTER TWELVE

The following morning, Toby yawned and rolled over onto his back. He'd slept fitfully on Old Joe's bed after an evening snuggled with Clarissa watching a Scandinavian horror movie. Normally, after a good gory movie, he'd sleep like a baby, but last night he'd found himself worrying about ... everything!

For starters, he'd had dreams about the hot air balloon getting a puncture and crash landing in a field full of hungry feral foxes, all named Frank. Then the dream had morphed into him leading all those foxes, who were kind of chasing him, but kind of following him, climbing the hill to Blackwell Manor. When they arrived there, the windows were in darkness, but he kept catching a glimpse of pairs of minuscule, shiny lights. He was certain the shiny things were eyes.

He'd lain awake for ages after that, trying to shake off his anxiety, but a non-stop stream of questions barraged his mind. Questions that even in the cold light of day he couldn't answer. Why had The Pointy Woman come back? Did she imagine she had unfinished business?

Is the unfinished business ... me?

Would Rory know why she'd suddenly arrived back in their lives? Or could he at least shed some light on possible reasons?

Grunting, Toby rolled over again. "Waah!" he shrieked. "What are you doing in here?" Sal was standing right at the tip of his snout. So close, in fact, Toby had to cross his eyes to keep focus.

"Sorry," Sal said, slicking down the fur on his head. "Did I make you jump?"

"What time is it?" Toby asked.

"A bit after six, I believe."

Toby yawned. "What are you doing awake at this time? I normally struggle to rouse you before midday."

Sal straightened his whiskers. "I am indeed a creature with nocturnal habits," he agreed. "And if I'm not much mistaken, so are 'edge'ogs."

Ah. That's what this was about. "Hedgehogs," Toby prompted Sal. "Huh huh huh huh."

"Huh?"

"We pronounce the ... Never mind." Toby lay his head down and closed his eyes. After lunch was still a long time away.

"Do you fink she likes me?" Sal asked.

Toby opened one eye. "Of course she does. She's a lovely lady and you're ..."

"I'm?"

"You're a ... you're ... Sal."

"Hmm." Sal didn't seem impressed with Toby's appraisal.

Toby sniffed. "Have you had a barf?"

"I snuck into the shower while Clarissa was washing her hair."

Toby almost fell off the bed. "You did what?"

Sal held out his front paw for inspection. "Coo! I smell gorgeous!"

Toby, against his better judgement, sniffed Sal's paw. He did smell fresh. Minty. "It's a good job she didn't see you, or there'd have been hell to pay."

"I know you think I'm an idiot, but that's why I wait until she's washing her hair! She keeps her eyes closed!"

"You've done it before?" Toby felt weak at the

knees. He didn't imagine Clarissa would be too pleased if she found out.

"I likes to be clean," said Sal, smoothing the fur on his head again. Toby had a sneaking suspicion Sal had used leave-in conditioner or gel or something to slick it down. "So, are you getting up or what?"

"*Or what*, probably. What's the rush?" Toby grumbled, but after huffing and moaning, he slid off the bed.

"I thought we could go for a run. Y'know? Maybe do a bit of a workout?" Sal flexed his muscles.

Toby choked back a laugh. "You're on your own, buddy."

"Why?" Sal asked, trailing after Toby as he pushed the bedroom door open slightly wider and led the way to the top of the stairs. "What are you going to do?"

"I'm going to start with breakfast, then I'm going to pay a cheeky visit to Mrs Crouch, and then"—Toby thought about the dreams he'd had—"I think I'm going to take myself for a walk in the park. There's someone I'd like to bump into."

At first, Toby thought he'd be out of luck. The day was still young—not even ten o'clock!—and until now, he'd only ever met Rory at lunchtime.

But as if by magick, Rory suddenly appeared at the park gates. Toby, dawdling near the children's swings—mainly to stay out of the way of the geese near the lake but also in the hope that some of the toddlers would drop their crisps or sweets—hurried over to meet him.

"Fancy meeting you here, lad!" Rory smiled and leaned over to pet Toby's ears.

"How did you know I'd be here this early?" Toby asked.

"I simply had a sense you would." Rory shrugged. "Did you want to see me?"

"I always want to see you, you should know that," said Toby.

"Let's stroll a little," Rory suggested. "I'm not so stiff this morning." He still walked with a pronounced limp though, Toby noticed. They began to promenade around Swan Lake, anti-clockwise. "Something on your mind?" Rory asked.

"The rain cut off our discussion about Miranda Dervish," Toby said. "I'd like to know more about her."

Rory remained mute for a while, simply kept

walking until he found a bench far away from anyone else. The park wasn't so busy this morning. It was a school day, and the serious early-morning joggers had already departed. The people jogging now were mums and older folk. There were some folk out with their dogs too, and a couple of teenagers skiving from school or college, but that was about it.

"That wind has a bit of a chill this morning," Rory said, taking a seat. The bench looked damp to Toby, but the old man didn't appear to mind. He didn't have his shopping bag with him. Nothing to fiddle with. He placed his gnarled hands in his lap.

"I hadn't noticed," said Toby. This wasn't strictly true. He'd been keeping an eye on the weather because he supposed if it was too rough, Hedda wouldn't fly. It's true there was a breeze, and yes, it felt cooler today, but nothing out of the ordinary. However, he didn't want to contradict Rory, so he added, "I don't think you feel it when you're low to the ground."

Rory chuckled. "Being a dog must have its advantages at times?"

"Lots of times," Toby agreed. But all this small talk was getting him nowhere. "Tell me more about ... *her*."

Rory twisted the side of his face. "You can't say her name either, can you?"

"What's her claim on Hightop Hall or Blackwell Manor or whatever it's called?" Toby asked. This was a long shot. He wasn't one hundred per cent certain The Pointy Woman had such a claim.

Rory inhaled sharply. "I thought I told you to stay away from there!"

"I have been staying away," Toby replied. That much was true. So far. "Is she related in some way to Madame Minovska?"

Rory's hands clenched into claws, his whole body becoming suddenly tense. "What do you know about *her*?"

Toby noted the old man's reaction and decided to play it down. "Not a lot. Clarissa found a book—"

"What book?"

"I don't remember the title. It was in the library. It mentioned a Madame Minovska who moved to Sun Valley from Russia and bought Blackwell Manor."

"She's been dead a long time," said Rory, the tension beginning to ease, his hands relaxing.

"We assumed that was the case, but Clarissa couldn't find out who owned the manor now, and given that I think The Pointy—I mean Miranda—is establishing her home there, we wondered if they were related in some way?"

"Who knows?" Rory smiled gently, his demeanour entirely different to how it had been a few moments before. "I'm not sure it's relevant."

"You're probably right," said Toby. "It seems odd, though—"

"I think you should put that house out of your mind, lad." Rory reached over and tickled behind Toby's ears. "It's an evil place. Forget it."

"But—"

Rory sighed. "I'll let you in on a secret, Toby. I wasn't planning to tell you this, but I can see that you're obsessed with ... the Dervish woman, and I understand that obsession completely. You're not the only one." He took a breath. "There exists a secret order who have been seeking her for many years."

A secret order? "Of wizards?" Toby asked.

"And witches. Demon hunters and the like."

Wowser! "It's a shame they didn't come and find her before she killed Old Joe."

"The problem they have is that she's notorious for assuming new identities. But not merely taking on a new name or moving to a new location—actually taking on an entirely fresh physicality."

Toby swallowed. "Is that possible?"

"It is if you're a shifter."

Toby's knees began to wobble. "But ... but ... if she's a shifter ... how would you ever know what she looked like? She could be hiding in plain sight?" He stared with fresh eyes at a jogger running past, her ponytail bouncing with each step. "She could be anyone. She could be a neighbour—"

"Or the neighbour's cat," Rory agreed.

Toby bit back a shriek of dismay. *She could be Moriarty! Or Sal!* How could he ever trust anyone or anything again?

"That's why I'm trying to tell you to stay away from the house," Rory reminded him. "Leave it to the experts. The ones who are better equipped to deal with her."

Toby stared at Rory, eyes wide. "Are you a member of that secret order?"

"It's better for you that you don't know anything, Toby. Trust me."

Toby licked his lips, thinking. "Okay. Does this secret order know that she may be living in the manor and that I think I've seen her recently?"

Rory nodded once.

"Okay." Toby's head was spinning. Yet more uncertainties. Rory might or might not be a member of this secret order, but he certainly knew enough about them to be able to confirm that they were looking into The Pointy Woman's whereabouts. That would have to be good enough.

"Go home, Toby," said Rory softly. "Be with Clarissa. Keep her safe." Rory pushed himself off the bench. "We shouldn't meet again."

He limped away, Toby staring after him, fighting feelings of awe and confusion, a million thoughts rioting in his mind. *If The Pointy Woman likes to shapeshift, then who or what can I trust? Will this secret order be capable of catching her even though they haven't before?* ***Why*** *haven't they before? What do they know? Anything? Nothing?*

Before Rory could leave the park, Toby was chasing after him. "Wait! Wait!" he barked, and a couple of young mothers grabbed their children and removed them from his path. "Wait, Rory. I have one more question."

Rory turned and paused at the gate, steadying himself against the stone pillar there.

"What does she want?" Toby asked. "Why is she back?"

"What does she want?" Rory repeated. "Everything, Toby. Everything."

CHAPTER THIRTEEN

"What's the matter with you?" Clarissa asked. "You've got a face like a wet weekend in Whitby."

"In where?" Toby asked, from where he was slumped on the sofa in the middle of a malaise.

"Whitby. It's in North Yorkshire. It's on the coast. Dracula stayed there." Clarissa was doing a spot of housework, which probably meant that Ed was coming around tonight. Either that or she had some work to do and she didn't want to get on with it.

Dracula? Toby's interest was piqued. "Have you been to this Whitby place?" he enquired.

"No, never."

"How do you know what a wet weekend in Whitby looks like then?" Toby asked, irritated now.

"I should imagine it's much the same as a wet weekend in Sun Valley, to be honest. Lots of people eating fish and chips by the sea with their hoods up." Clarissa tossed her duster onto the dining room table, all the better to smush his ears between her warm palms. "What's up?"

"Nothing," Toby lied. From his vantage point he could see out of the big front window. Moriarty was sitting on his gatepost cleaning her face. The sky had started to cloud over and the wind had gathered pace. Every now and again, a single splash of rain would smash against the windowpane.

All Toby could think about was that Moriarty might not be who she said she was. How could he know?

"I don't believe you," said Clarissa. "Shall we have some lunch?"

"Okay." Even lunch didn't fill Toby with much enthusiasm.

Clarissa felt his nose. "Are you under the weather?"

Such a strange expression, thought Toby. *How can you be under the weather when you're indoors?* "I'm fine." As much as he loved Clarissa, he had a sudden urge to evade her scrutiny. "I'm going to nip outside and have a chat with Moriarty."

"Okay. I'm making cheese on toast, so don't be too long."

Toby heaved himself from the sofa and out into the kitchen. After a few laps of water from his bowl, he slunk through the dog flap and around the side of the house. Part of him wanted Moriarty to disappear before he made it to the gate so he wouldn't have to confront her, but she was still there when he arrived.

"Good afternoon," Moriarty purred, washing behind her left ear. Her fur shone beautifully, but not as bright as her luminous green eyes. Whenever Toby stopped to pay proper attention to her, he had to admit she was a beautiful cat. His meticulous scrutiny did not evade her notice. "Why are you looking at me like that?" she asked, turning those shining headlights on him.

Toby blinked. "You know, I don't think I've ever seen you with your hoomans," he said.

Moriarty studied him. "I wouldn't be seen dead with any hooman. I'm not a dog." She pronounced this last word with total disdain. "I don't need a handler."

"Honestly? I find it a bit odd, that's all." Toby

shrugged. "Maybe you don't belong to them. Maybe you're a stray."

"Do you think I'm a liar?" Moriarty crouched on the post. She came across as relaxed, but Toby knew she could spring in any direction in a nanosecond. Including at his face. "What difference would it make if I was a stray?" Moriarty hissed. "What do you have against them?"

"I don't have anything against them," Toby hurried to say. "One of my best friends is a stray."

"I haven't seen Pippin lately, so maybe she's gone off you," Moriarty pointed out. "Are you struggling to keep your friends, Toby? Even your best ones?"

"No. I—"

"Because with an attitude like yours, it wouldn't surprise me in the slightest." Moriarty's tone was mild, but by goodness, the accompanying glare cut Toby to shreds.

"I'm sure you're absolutely who you say you are —" Toby tried to explain.

"You're sure?" Moriarty spat. "I'm thrilled to be blessed with your gracious certainty."

"It's not like that—"

"Pffffffft!" came Moriarty's final response before she leapt from the gatepost and shot across the road and under a hedge.

Oh.

"That didn't go well." Sal peeped out from beneath a nearby bush.

"Are you spying on me?" Toby asked crossly.

"Not at all, guv! Not at all. I saw you comin' out and I followed you cos I was wantin' to know what time we're leavin'. That cat scares me to death, though. Fierce she is. Fierce!" He came all the way out so that Toby could see him.

"What are you wearing around your neck?" Toby asked.

"It's a wool tie. I knitted it. Whaddayathink?"

Apart from a dropped stitch here and there, it wasn't bad at all for a first attempt. "Why are you wearing a tie?" Toby wanted to know.

"I thought Hedda might like it?" Sal pretended to box. Ducking and diving and throwing out his clenched paws.

"I'm sure she'll be impressed." Toby shook his head. "Boy, you've got it bad."

"She's a total peach, that Hedda. An' she's going places. Don't ya think?"

Toby tipped his head back to examine the sky. "She might not be going anywhere today. And neither will we."

"Such little faith, guv." Sal smoothed the fur on

his head. Despite his best attempts this morning with the hair gel or whatever he'd borrowed from Clarissa, his fur spiked this way and that in its usual unkempt fashion.

Toby pondered over Sal. He couldn't imagine for a moment that The Pointy Woman would turn herself into a cowardly fat rat who enjoyed knitting and bathing and eating tuna treats. Wouldn't she want to reach for better than that?

And yet, what better way to worm yourself into someone's life than to pull on their heartstrings, share a sob story and be absolutely pathetic so that Toby's only response would be to take you under his wing and keep you close?

Sal knew everything. It would be mighty clever of The Pointy Woman to pull that off.

"So, what time we leavin'?"

"Soon," said Toby, trying to shake off his sudden feelings of paranoia. "Let's have a spot of lunch first. I'll need to think of something to tell Clarissa before we go ..."

CHAPTER FOURTEEN

"Hey, buddies!" Frank met them at the entrance to the woods. They hadn't arranged to meet and so it came as a bit of a surprise—especially for Sal, who nearly fell off Toby's back. But at least this time he didn't faint.

"How are you doin'?" he asked Frank.

Frank bounced around like a puppy—or a kit—and wagged his great brush. "Excited!" he said. "What about you fellas?"

"I'm excited too!" said Sal, although in his case it was less because of the balloon ride and more because of seeing Hedda again. "You'll have to ignore Toby—he's in a funny mood."

"I'm not in a funny mood," Toby replied, but even so, he examined Frank for any signs that might indicate he could be The Pointy Woman in disguise. Frank was pretty sleek and his nose was pointy, but apart from that—and his bright orange eyes that had a tendency to burn right through you—there was nothing to suggest he might be a shapeshifter.

Aowwww! I'm so confused, thought Toby.

Frank began to lead them through the woods. Toby imagined that had Frank not been here, it wouldn't be too much of a problem—Toby could simply follow their scent trail from the previous day —but Frank *had* been invited along on this trip, and it would be churlish of Toby to uninvite him now. Besides, the fox was thrilled about having friends to do something with.

Now and then, Frank would peek back or wait for Toby and Sal to catch him up. Eventually, he nudged Toby with his nose. "Are you sure you're alright?"

"I wish people would stop asking me that," Toby snapped. "I'm perfectly fine!"

"Maybe he's scared of flying," Sal suggested, as though Toby wasn't right there underneath him.

"I'm not afraid of heights," said Toby.

"But heights aren't the same as flying," Sal told him.

Annoyingly, Sal had a point.

"Have you eaten something that disagreed with you?" Frank asked. "I once ate half a dozen cabbages at one sitting, and I swear I wasn't right for weeks."

"Raw?" asked Sal.

"Oh, yes," said Frank.

Sal's eyes widened. "Impressive. I bet you were proper windy!"

"Why did you eat half a dozen cabbages?" Toby asked.

"I wanted to find out whether I'd make a good vegetarian," Frank told him. "Sadly, I wouldn't."

"Oooh." Sal leaned away from Frank, grimacing. "I almost forgot you were a carbivore."

"Carnivore," Toby corrected him.

"What's a carbivore?" Frank asked.

"Someone who likes potatoes, probably," Toby decided.

"Whoop!" Sal punched the air. "Chips and crisps for the win!"

Toby agreed, his spirits beginning to lift. "With salt and vinegar on the chips!"

"Nom!" said Sal.

Frank laughed at their enthusiasm. "I've never had chips or crisps."

"Mate, you ain't lived," Sal told him. "We'll have to bring you some. Never mind being a carnivore!

After you've tasted the joy on a discarded tray that is chips, you'll be a carbivore for the rest of your life."

Laughing together, the three of them resumed their journey, hardly noticing the rain beginning to fall harder onto the canopy of trees above their heads. It only became apparent when they arrived at the Sow by Sow-west clearing.

The first thing they noticed was that Hedda had inflated the balloon. The bright pink and muted purple of the silk, once inflated, took over much of the available space and was a whole lot phoofier than they'd been expecting.

The second thing they noticed was the thunking of the raindrops on the balloon's taut skin.

Toby heard the distinct sound of a mallet on wood. Hedda was around the other side of the balloon, tightening the guylines that kept it moored to the ground.

"Hi, Hedda!" Frank called.

"Hey, boys!" Hedda emerged from around the side looking virtually unrecognisable. It wasn't the miniature pilot goggles that changed her appearance so much as the teeny corks. Resembling mini wine corks, they'd been painted neon yellow at the ends. There were hundreds of them, each one stuck on the end of one of her prickles.

"Whoa!" Sal gawped in horror and tumbled from Toby's back.

"What's all that?" Toby asked, leaning closer to Hedda for a sniff.

"Oh, don't mind me!" Hedda giggled, pushing him away. "I have to wear these corks otherwise I pop the envelope."

"The what now?" Toby asked, looking around for inflatable stationery.

"The envelope. That's what you call the blowy-up bit of the balloon. I'm very good at puncturing it, and trust me, that's not something you want happening mid-flight."

"Ha ha." Toby laughed nervously.

"That's a good point, that is!" Sal recovered himself. "You're a proper genius, you are, Miss Hedda."

"It takes me forever to get ready," Hedda added. "That's why I only do afternoon flights."

"Ah." Toby turned his attention to the *envelope*. Now that it was inflated and he was so close to it, he was experiencing some heebie-geebies. *Is this thing safe?* "All fixed, is it?" He purposefully kept his voice light. All of a sudden, the bicycle didn't seem such a bad method of transport after all. *How high does this thing go?* Toby wondered and swallowed. *Are there any parachutes?*

A close-up examination proved there wasn't much to the balloon itself. To Toby's untrained eye, it looked like ordinary silk that had been treated with something to make it tougher. The basket might have been purchased from a farmer's market as something to carry your vegetables home in. Added to this, there was some sort of frame-contraption-thingie inside, hanging between the envelope and the basket, that blew the hot air into the belly of the balloon. It burned with a blue flame.

Yoikes!

Already taking space in the basket were what appeared to be bags of sand—the ballast, perhaps—and a fire extinguisher. It would be a snug fit for a fox, a dog, a rat and a hedgehog.

Ouch! Those corks are going to be game-changers, after all!

"Yes, all fixed and ready to go." Hedda pulled at one of the guylines, checking the tension. "One minor problem, boys."

Toby perked up. *What? We can't go? Such a shame!*

"I am concerned about the weather," Hedda

confessed. "I don't mind a smattering of rain and a bit of wind, but nothing too excessive."

Toby exchanged glances with Frank and Sal. Funnily enough, both of them looked somewhat green around the gills. Were they as sick to the stomach as he was?

"It would be a terrific shame if we couldn't go," mumbled Sal, but he wasn't fooling Toby, who'd seen that look on Sal's face often enough to know that the rat might faint at any moment.

"I'm not saying no," said Hedda, bustling around, busily checking knobs and ropes and tension and slack and ... stuff.

"If you think it's dangerous ..." Toby shrugged. "Who are we to say otherwise?"

"I do hate to disappoint my clients, though," Hedda said, and darted into her hollow log.

Frank grimaced. "I've never even climbed a tree," he whispered to Toby.

Toby thought of his wizard shack and how he liked to sit on the roof. "I've made it about eight feet off the ground," he said. "Not much more than that."

Sal, bless his heart, fled behind a bush and quietly disposed of his lunch.

Hedda, now wearing a yellow hi-vis waistcoat as well as the corks, returned with a tray of drinks.

"Blackberry and ginger tea," she announced. "Good for steadying the nerves." She surveyed her wan passengers. "And the stomach."

"We're definitely going, then?" Toby asked.

"I think we'll risk it," said Hedda. "The forecast mentioned light rain, so I think we've had the worst of it."

"Ohhhhhh," groaned Sal, reaching a shaking paw for his tea.

"Super," said Frank, and downed his tea in one.

"Fantastic," said Toby, forcing a wag as he sipped his own tea.

Thus fortified, Hedda instructed Frank to jump into the basket first. "And if you hold on to Sal for a moment—"

"You what?" Sal took a step back. "I'm not sure—"

"You'll be fine, little man," said Frank. "Didn't I promise?"

"You did, but—"

"Mush, mush!" sang Hedda. "We want to make the best of the available light, don't we?"

Reluctantly, Sal climbed into the basket and allowed Frank to hold on to him. This gave Toby enough room to squeeze in, leaving Hedda till last. She began to pull pegs and the balloon lifted a little.

"Whoa there," she said, patting the basket on its side as though it were a recalcitrant horse that would do as she told it. Round the basket she trotted, pulling pegs one by one until only one remained.

The balloon fought to escape, straining at its one remaining tie.

"Groooooooo," mumbled Sal, and grabbed hold of the edge of the basket so he could lean over.

"Okay, Toby," Hedda called. "I want you to help me into the basket as I pull out this final peg, then we'll lose some of our ballast and see how we go."

"Rightio!" Toby shouted back, adrenaline flooding his veins and eradicating his jitters. He angled himself over the basket, bracing his hind paws. "I'm ready!"

"Let's do it!"

Toby reached for Hedda, yanking her up by the back of her vest. As she left the ground, she hauled on the final peg and it came away. The balloon lurched, throwing Toby back into Frank, who collapsed under his weight. Toby landed on top of him with Hedda on his belly.

"Whoopsadaisy!" Hedda said, as cheerful as ever. "We're climbing, boys!"

Toby fought to get to his feet. It wasn't easy. He wasn't sure which of the tangle of legs belonged to him and which to Frank. They exchanged apologies: "So sorry", "Ooh, I do beg your pardon," "My mistake", but eventually, he hauled himself upright and peered over the side. They'd risen a good twelve feet or so.

"We need to drop some ballast," Hedda said and began hauling a number of bags of sand from the bottom of the basket and throwing them overboard, where they landed safely in the clearing.

"Would you like me to get rid of a couple?" asked Toby, striving to be helpful. He picked one and launched it over the edge with slightly too much rigour. It clunked into a nearby oak tree and startled a pair of blackbirds who exploded into the air, loudly protesting the disturbance.

"Ooops!" Toby hoisted another bag of sand but, this time, dropped it directly down.

Frank, eager to be of assistance too, also began throwing ballast overboard.

Perhaps, between them, they overdid it. Suddenly the balloon rocketed upwards, and once again, Frank and Toby lost their balance.

"Ow!"

"Sorry! Sorry! Oof!"

"I do beg your pardon. Again."

"It's okay. Eurgh."

Toby dragged himself upright, his head fizzing with the sudden upward velocity. "Wowser!" he said. "I didn't know the balloon came equipped with turbo boosters."

"It doesn't," said Hedda, and for the first time, Toby thought he could hear a trace of worry. "The wind up here is stronger than I thought it would be. We seem to have found a thermal."

"A thermal?" Toby scanned his surroundings but couldn't see anyone wearing a vest. Or a scarf for that matter. That reminded him. "Where's Sal?" he asked.

"Isn't he here?" Hedda, busy doing something mechanical with the gas and flame, shot a panicked look at her feet.

"He must be." Frank sifted through the odds and ends on the floor of the basket, the few remaining bags of sand, the fire extinguisher and some more hi-vis vests. When his search yielded no sign of the fat rat, Toby became seriously worried and started to join in.

"Sal? Sal!" he yelled. "Where are you?"

"He's not here," Frank said.

Toby reared away from the fox in alarm. "You haven't eaten him, have you?"

"What?" Frank clutched a paw to his chest and threw himself against the side of the basket. "No!"

"Did you mistake him for ballast and throw him overboard?"

"No!"

"Let's all calm down here," ordered Hedda. "You're rocking the boat, boys!"

She meant literally; the basket swayed from side to side so that everyone had to find a way to hold on.

"Help." The tiniest of voices.

"Did you hear that?" Frank asked.

"Helllp!"

"Where's it coming from?" Toby crouched down, starting to search through everything again. The basket lurched once more, throwing Frank against the side.

"Hellllllllp!"

"Eeek!" Frank caught his breath. "Holy moly!"

"What is it?" Hedda asked.

Toby jumped to his feet and squeezed alongside Frank. Most of the weight of the basket was now on the same side. The basket tipped.

"Waaaaaah!" Hedda cried, desperately trying to cope with the gas, the wind and the lack of stability.

Toby peeked over the side of the basket. Terra firma was a long, long way below. He could see the whole wood—the tree tops sharp or round, sparse or bushy—in all its multicoloured glory. A zillion shades of green, many fading and mixed with the hues of autumn; the reds and browns, the golds and silvers, the oranges and purples. Nature's glorious pallet.

And beyond the woods was Bushy Leaze, with its winding lanes and big houses, the picturesque church and a pub. \

Had he examined the terrain more carefully, Toby would certainly have spotted his friend Sparky's house, and he might even have seen Sparky in the garden shouting at something only he could hear.

But no. Because Toby was staring aghast at a flying rat.

Sal wasn't genuinely flying. Not in the I-have-wings-and-I-am-flapping-them-and-floating-through-the-air sense of the word, but he did have tight hold of a thin piece of rope tethered to the basket that might once have been tied to a peg.

At some stage, Sal had fallen out without anyone noticing.

"Oh, my dogness!" Toby reached down to see if he could catch hold of the rope, but it was about eight inches out of reach. "Frank?" Toby called over his shoulder. "You're going to have to catch hold of me and help lower me down enough that I can reach the rope."

"That's going to be difficult," Frank said. "We're about the same weight."

"I'll help!" said Hedda. "I'm as strong an ox." There could be no denying this.

Toby had an idea. "Is there any more rope?"

"There is!" Hedda pointed upwards. Ropes, attached to the frame, were coiled in several places. She made a grab for one and offered it to Toby.

"Great!" Toby placed one end in his mouth and stepped towards Frank.

"Helllllllllp!" Sal cried again.

"We're coming!" shouted Hedda. "Hold on!"

"What are you doing?" Frank regarded Toby with suspicion and backed away.

"I need to tie you up," said Toby through the mouthful of rope.

"Why?"

"You'll manage my weight more easily if you can't come loose yourself," Toby explained. "Don't worry. I'll untie you once we've rescued Sal."

"Hellllllllllllllllllp!"

"We need to hurry!" Hedda urged.

"Alright! Do it!" cried Frank.

"Stand there!" Toby directed the fox and then

muttered a quick spell. "*Alligant*!" The rope snaked out of his mouth and around Frank's body, knotting itself in complicated ways until Frank was securely tied, but with enough room to manoeuvre himself and stretch.

"Help. Oh, help me, please!" Sal pleaded. "I can't hold on much longer! My paws are so tired!"

"I'm coming!" cried Toby, and climbed onto the edge of the basket. Frank grabbed a leg and clamped down. A little too hard. His teeth were sharp!

Toby didn't complain, however. He was too focused on Sal to worry. He slithered down the side of the basket, the claws on his front paws catching on it and helping to slow down his descent. He didn't need to drop too far before he was able to grab the rope tether with his mouth and lift Sal. "Pull us up!" Toby called, his mouth full.

Frank heaved, and Sal finally came level with the basket. "More!" squeaked Sal, his soft voice almost lost, blown away by the wind.

Frank pulled again, and now Toby could lock his back legs against the basket. With a wiggle and a wriggle and an *oomph!* he and Sal dropped into the basket and collapsed against the base. Toby lay panting. He wasn't sure he'd managed to breathe at all during the rescue mission. On his chest, Sal shivered with cold.

"I-i-iy-iy-iy-iy-iy thought I was a goner," he said, teeth chattering.

"I thought you were too!" spluttered Hedda.

"Me three," said Toby.

"Thank goodness we heard you!" said Frank.

"I couldn't have held on for much longer," Sal said, as close to tears as Toby had ever seen him.

"So brave," said Hedda, throwing her arms around Sal and kissing his forehead.

"Cor," said Sal.

Hedda smiled at him.

Sal flushed.

"So brave," said Hedda.

"It was nothing. Honestly!" said Sal. "My commando training coming in useful, that's all."

Toby rolled his eyes. *Commando training, my furry backside,* he thought, but he would never be so mean as to ruin Sal's big moment with Hedda, so he kept his thoughts firmly to himself and made a big show of picking himself up and peering out at the landscape while Hedda and Sal giggled together like schoolkids.

The balloon was being blown slightly inland, so that was good news and, according to Toby's reckoning—no grand mariner, he—they were heading east, away from the sun. Not that the sun was out and about, but you could tell where it was hiding behind the clouds if you scrunched your face and squinted.

Sun Valley lay behind them. Seatown—presumably that's what it was—to the right. Beyond that, somewhere in the hills, they'd find Blackwell Manor.

"We're on course!" Toby cried, full of excitement now that the drama had passed.

"That's good news." Hedda left Sal's side and scrambled up the basket, grabbing hold of a rope to help her keep her balance. She surveyed the landscape and tsked.

"What's the matter?" Toby asked.

"Not happy with those clouds." Hedda pointed out the black sky behind them.

"Maybe they won't catch us up," said Toby.

"Let's hope not," said Hedda and swung down to check on Sal.

"Excuse me," called Frank. "Excuse me?"

Toby glanced over his shoulder.

"I hate to be a nuisance," said the fox. "But could you possibly untie me now?"

CHAPTER FIFTEEN

Gliding through the air so high above the ground was a mighty peculiar feeling. Toby couldn't work out whether his brain or his stomach was more perturbed. For the most part, so far—bar when they'd been searching for Sal—the trip had been smooth. The wind—though high—and the air—pretty nippy—were at acceptable levels. Plus the quiet up here, away from the roads, and the birds come to that, was truly phenomenal.

An occasional seagull or kestrel flew by and eyed them suspiciously, but apart from that, nothing disturbed their progress.

With one eye firmly on the horizon, there could be no doubting that they were heading in the right direction. The problem was that *behind* them, the clouds were giving chase. And rather than the fluffy, white, friendly clouds of a children's bedtime storybook, these were big, black and full of anger.

Toby had been fixated on the view in front of him, seeking the slightest advance peek of Blackwell Manor. He supposed the manor would be difficult to identify, surrounded as it was by trees. They probably wouldn't catch their first sight of it until they were almost directly above it. Occasionally he worried that they must have been blown off course, but when he checked the sea view and the position of Seatown, he accepted that they hadn't.

The balloon lurched.

"What was that?" Frank asked, the whites of his eyes showing.

"Nothing to worry about," said Hedda, but from the look on her face, Toby suspected she was telling porky pies.

From somewhere far behind them came a deep, menacing boom.

"What was that?" Frank asked again, but this time his voice had risen three octaves.

Hedda peered back the way they'd come. "Oh," she said.

"Oh?" Toby turned, curious to see what she was looking at. He half expected an aeroplane or something to be bearing down on them, but there was nothing but the clouds. They did seem to be much closer than they had been before.

And so incredibly dark, thought Toby. *Brooding almost—*

Toby caught his breath as a streak of bright light forked out of the cloud bank.

"Wha—?" He got no further. The booming came again.

"It's a storm," said Hedda, albeit unnecessarily. They were all clearly aware of that now. "We can outrun it. Not far to go—"

With that, the heavens opened.

"Should we be flying in a storm?" Frank asked, his voice quavering.

Toby hated Frank for asking the question, even though his knees were knocking too.

"If Miss Hedda thinks we'll be fine, then we'll be fine," said Sal, with a self-conscious air of bravado.

"Of course," said Toby and swallowed his nerves, facing forward once more. Everywhere he looked, the sky around them had grown heavier, and visibility had been reduced to virtually nothing. He concentrated on a lighter patch of ground way ahead of them where the storm had yet to reach.

"There!" he shouted.

Boom!

The noise exploded around them, so thunderous that Toby imagined his eardrums had burst. He dropped to the bottom of the basket, holding his paws over his ears. Rainwater flooded down the sides of the envelope and, although most of it was directed over the curves and down towards the ground, enough of it found its way into the basket to drench the four animals.

"Did you see it?" Hedda shouted. "The manor?"

"Yes!" Toby hauled himself upright once more and peered out into the gathering gloom. The light had failed so dismally that he could imagine what flying by night would be like. He took a second to get his bearings before locating his target. "Over there!" he directed Hedda. "See?"

A long, growling rumble filled the sky. It rolled around them for what seemed an eternity before fading away, and then the following moment, *Boom!*

Lightning flashed and the balloon jolted sideways.

"Meep!" Hedda swung onto a rope and climbed up to take a peep. "I don't like this," she yelled, coming back down. "I think we may well have taken a hit there."

"Listen," bellowed Toby. "I'm no pilot, but if you think we should land, I say go for it—"

A gust of wind grabbed them and tossed them backwards.

"I think we should," Hedda agreed, the only creature in the basket who could keep her balance.

Boom!

Toby cowered, the rainwater running down his back.

Beside him, Frank, thoroughly miserable, his fur slicked down and raindrops sparkling on his whiskers, hunched his shoulders. "Remind me never to do this again," he whispered.

"And if you catch *me* wanting to, you have my permission to put me out of my misery," Toby whispered back. "I think I'm done with all forms of transportation ..."

"This day was a complete waste of hair conditioner," Sal said, desperately trying to wring the water out of his fur. But then he noticed Hedda, valiantly trying to keep the balloon on course. "Well, almost."

"Toby," Hedda called above the roar of the wind. "Take another look for me. The rain is making it difficult to see—"

Toby fought his way up, the wind tugging at his

ears, making them flap, the rain, now horizontal, stinging his eyes. He blinked into the distance, searching ... searching ...

"There!" he shouted. "It's closer now! Look!"

Hedda leaned against him and followed his paw.

"The chimneys are poking above the trees!" said Toby.

"Is there a clear spot? Anywhere we can put this thing down?" Hedda asked, turning her attention to the balloon's flame.

"There's parking for cars," Toby called. "And there's a back garden. But I'm not sure we should get that close—"

Boom!

The noise of a thousand bass drums exploded around them. The basket skipped forwards and backwards as though it were dancing. Then—

Fzzzzzzzzzzzzzzzzzzzzzz!

Bright blue-white lightning ripped the sky asunder, and the balloon dropped like a stone.

Everyone on board screamed.

Including Hedda.

"Oh no no no no no," she said, pulling herself together and grabbing her controls. The balloon jerked as it stopped its descent. "Don't you be doing this to me. Don't you—"

The wind whooshed and the balloon flew sideways, tilting in such a fashion that everyone would have been ejected if they hadn't already been holding on for dear life.

"Waaaaaaaaah!"

"I feel like I've lost control!" shouted Hedda. "I shouldn't have, but I can't do anything—"

"Let's just land!" cried Toby.

Hedda nodded and began pulling on levers and twisting knobs. The gas feed to the flame started to diminish, but it was too little, too late. The next bolt of lightning struck the balloon's canopy and the wind grabbed them with strong, determined hands.

"We're going down!" cried Hedda. "I'm so, so sorry!"

Sssssssssssssssssssss.

As the balloon began to deflate above them, Frank and Toby exchanged glances. Hedda and Sal touched noses, and Hedda closed her eyes.

Toby imagined they would plummet to the earth to become strawberry jam on a country lane somewhere, but their descent was nothing like that. The wind kept them in its tight grip, dragging them sideways. Sure, they were dropping, but not at a catastrophic rate.

"Oh, my goodness!" Toby peered over the basket. The manor hove into view.

Frank joined him. "We're going to land in front of that old building."

"That's the manor! If we land there, it will rather give the game away," said Toby. "I was hoping to remain incognito."

"Don't worry." Hedda had dared to open her eyes. "I think we're on course to fly straight over it!"

"You may be right!" Toby examined the drop. They must have been thirty or forty feet above the tallest trees here. The wind would push them over and they would land either in the back garden, or perhaps in the field beyond.

Good news!

The balloon swooped and dropped as though nestling in the hands of some outsized entity. Toby goggled at the vista before them. The manor taking shape in front of his eyes. Not only the chimneys but also the red tiles on the roof, the scaffolding on the side of the house. The cream stone of the walls. The vehicles parked beside the barn. The gables ...

"Oooo-er!" Toby wanted to hide his eyes but he couldn't look away. Another roll of thunder and a blinding flash of light. In the immediate—oddly silent—aftermath, the wind dropped—and so, of course, did the balloon.

"Oh no," muttered Hedda.

"We can still clear it!" said Frank, urging the balloon on through his will alone.

"We won't make it!" Hedda wailed.

"Levitate the balloon!" Sal squeaked. "You can do it, Toby!"

For a moment Toby imagined he could, but even as he conjured the idea, he knew it wouldn't work. The basket alone was too heavy for him, let alone its occupants and the kit used to fly it.

"I can't!" Toby stared aghast as the manor began to dominate the whole of his view.

Frank grimaced, half turning away. "We're going to smash into the wall!"

"No, no—" Hedda shrieked.

So close now, Toby could clearly see the pointing on the building filling the space between the bricks. It needed redoing.

He winced as the wall came closer. Three. Two. O—

At the very last moment, a sudden updraft of wind lifted the balloon by a few feet. For one happy moment, he imagined they would clear the roof, but it wasn't quite enough. The half-inflated balloon stalled at the highest point, unable to clear the ridge. The basket became trapped, hanging there for a nanosecond before it began to slide backwards.

Everyone shrieked.

In slow motion, the basket, now resting on the roof, began to slip and slide like some untethered rollercoaster from a nightmare. Toby gripped hold of the rim, although he knew that wouldn't do any good at all. Not where they were going.

The basket hit the guttering and paused there briefly, but gravity and its backward trajectory meant that the only destination was down.

It tilted on its axis, threatening to spill its creature contents ...

"Ohmylifeohmylifeohmylife!" chanted Frank, cringing in the corner.

Sal squeaked and fainted dead away.

Hedda, holding tight to the central unit with one paw, raised the other in a defiant fist. A captain going down with her ship.

Toby conjured an image of Old Joe, beautiful and shining and smiling, his hands soft and loving as they reached for his pup. *Here I come*, Toby told the image. *Wait for me.*

Nothing happened.

Well ... nothing happened except that thunder

continued to roll and the lightning streaked through the sky and the rain came down in icy torrents and the wind gusted from the side and from above *and* from below.

The basket shuddered and creaked, but it held fast.

Toby's eyes met Hedda's.

"What's going on?" Hedda mouthed.

Toby shook his head. *No idea.*

Hedda used the central frame to climb higher. With the basket tilted to the side with the drop, she found herself at a difficult angle and had to balance her weight awkwardly, but she managed to manoeuvre herself to a position where she could see.

"The envelope is snagged on a chimney!" she called.

Frank stared at her wide-eyed, then whooped. "We're saved!"

Sal opened his eyes. "We're saved?"

"I wouldn't say that," was Hedda's flat response.

"Why?" asked Toby, unsure whether he wanted to hear the answer or not.

"The silk isn't going to hold," said Hedda. "We need to—"

She didn't finish.

Zuuzzzzzzzzzzp!

The material began to rip.

The basket dropped.

Hedda began to tumble.

Frank shrieked.

Sal fainted again.

Toby reached for his image of Old Joe.

CHAPTER SIXTEEN

Weirdly, in an emergency, time often becomes elastic. It can be bent and stretched like bubblegum. It possesses a kind of magick.

Here, floating in a wicker basket fifty or more feet above the ground, held in place by a couple of threads that some kind of butterfly-wormy thing once pooped out, Toby was glad of this fact.

Because ... as Hedda began to fall, even as he reached for the comforting image of his first hooman, he tapped into his own magick instead. Without properly thinking about it, he imagined headbutting Hedda into an open goal. She immediately altered trajectory, rolling into a protective ball—albeit slightly hampered by the corks—and, instead of bouncing on the side of the wicker basket and tumbling to the earth far below, his 'football' hit the crossbar. Hedda flipped back over the other side of the basket and landed on the roof.

Boink, boink, boink.

She landed in the guttering beside the basket and came to a stop.

As did the basket.

The balloon material had torn, but it still held.

"We have to get out!" Toby cried. "Now!"

"The basket's at the wrong angle," Frank told him, frantically trying to shift the balance by putting more weight on the side closest to the roof. "We can't climb out."

"We don't have a choice!" Toby said. "You can go first. You'll need to climb over the highest end of the basket. Make use of your claws. Once you get onto the roof, you're going to have to hold the basket steady so that I can climb over too, otherwise the imbalance of weight may send me plummeting."

Frank laughed weakly.

"And that would never do," Toby reminded him.

Frank nodded. "Never a truer word spoken."

"What about me?" Sal squeaked, having apparently come to again.

"You can climb this easily!" said Toby. "It's child's play for a rat!"

"I'm not so sure." Sal rubbed his tummy nervously.

Frank nudged him. "Miss Hedda's waiting for you on the other side ..."

"She is?" Sal's pale face came awake.

"She needs your help," Toby added.

"She does?"

"Yep." Toby jerked his head towards the side of the basket, but Sal was already moving. He wasn't the most graceful of rats, although he may have been the biggest and the most melodramatic, but he could climb when he needed to and, let's face it, he absolutely needed to now.

Once he'd made it over, Toby nodded at Frank.

Frank grimaced, but he knew what he needed to do. As Toby leaned all of his weight against the side of the basket, Frank began to climb. He scrambled, using the ridges in the wicker to gain some footholds, but the angle of the basket looked set to defeat him. Toby stretched his back up, driving as much force as he could through his legs to try and maintain his balance. "Use my back!" he shouted as the wind whipped against them. He felt Frank's hind paws gently scratch his back, then the fox's whole weight as he pushed hard ... then the weight had gone and the basket rocked and became incredibly light.

"Your turn, Toby!" Frank yelled. "We're holding the basket!"

Toby couldn't see any of his friends. The wind gusted. The basket wobbled. The rain blew into his eyes. He had to trust in the three creatures he'd started this journey with. What other choice did he have? "Hold tight," he begged, and stepped back. Beneath him, one edge of the basket hung over the void. He took a step and leapt for the opposite edge. Thanks to luck more than his unerring judgement, his front paws made it, although the rest of him didn't. As his body obeyed gravity and he started to fall backwards, he dug his paws into the wicker and swung in mid-air like a gymnast. Once. Twice. Then, when his rump swung out the third time, he hauled himself up and over the edge before leaping onto the roof, landing with a soft crump and smacking his not-quite-healed chin on the tiles.

Ooof! That'th hurty!

"You did it!" shrieked Hedda, beaming over at him, water dripping from her goggles. "Woohoo!"

Toby turned to see her gripping hold of a rope tether, a half-drowned Sal beside her. Frank had his teeth in the actual basket and was trying to extricate himself.

Zuuzzzzzzzzzzp!

"That's the silk done for!" Hedda let go of her rope at the same moment as Frank freed himself. Toby recognised the danger instantly. The basket, teetering on the edge, held there only by a wish and a song ... and Sal ... alone and still gripping his tether.

"Let go!" Toby bellowed at Sal. Before poor confused Sal had time to react, Frank, seeing what was about to happen, jumped towards him and swiped him into his mouth. For one horrible moment, Toby thought Sal would keep holding on and that he and Frank would follow the basket as it careered to the ground. Right in the nick of time, however, Sal threw his rope away as though he'd been holding a cobra, and he and Frank cowered at the edge of the roof, watching as the basket dropped away.

An interminable amount of time seemed to pass between the basket tottering over the guttering and the sound of it smashing into pieces below.

Hedda bowed her head. "Rest in peace," she said, removing her goggles and rubbing her eyes.

Toby tried to lighten the mood. "I think you mean rest in pieces."

"That too." Hedda fanned her face, blinking back tears. "There goes my business."

Frank placed Sal gently down and shook himself. "We'll help you get started again."

"Absolutely," said Toby. "I feel like it's all my fault. If it hadn't been for me, you wouldn't have been making this trip today at all!"

"No." Hedda shook her head and removed her hi-vis jacket. "Forget it. I think I've had enough of ballooning to last me a lifetime. I'll have to try my paw at something else."

Sal, busily wiping himself down, pulling faces and muttering "Fox spit" to himself, suddenly jerked upright. "How are we goin' to get off this roof?" he asked. "Please don't tell me we're goin' to abseil, because I am totally done with heights!"

"Sssssssh!" Frank crouched, ears pricked, studying the landscape below.

"Wassup?" Sal dived between Frank's paws.

"Company," whispered Frank.

Hedda and Toby crept towards the edge of the roof, huddling close to Frank. Headlights were travelling along the lane towards the manor.

"No-one's going to see us hiding out on the roof," whispered Hedda.

"Vehicles are coming and going all day," Toby told them. "They're doing the place up."

"Would that explain why there's a convoy then?" Frank asked.

Toby peered down the lane. It wouldn't be dark for a few hours yet, but the weather made for poor visibility. Besides the horizontal rain, the black clouds and the thunder—which were now beginning to move away—a sea mist had started to creep inland. Three sets of headlights floated along the lane. "I guess so," he said, but as they huddled together, dripping wet, watching the vehicles drift ever closer, Toby realised these weren't contractors; these were cars. Identical black cars, rather like the government ones he'd seen during Sun Valley's zombie outbreak.

I don't like this, he thought.

"Let's find a way to get off this roof," he said, fighting not to show his alarm. "And when we do, we need to take care. We don't want to be seen."

Hedda peeked over the edge, directly downwards. "Someone's bound to spot the remains of the balloon, aren't they?"

"Paws crossed, they don't." Toby gestured to the right. "I have an idea. This way. Mind how you go."

He led them across the roof. Sal slithered on a tile and it scooted out from under his foot. He skated in mid-air for a moment, like an extra in a Scooby-Doo cartoon. "Eeek!" He clutched his heart as Hedda put out a steadying paw.

"Watch out for loose tiles," said Frank, bringing up the rear, and giggled.

"It's not only that they're loose, they're wet as well!" Hedda said, holding on to Sal as she followed Toby. Sal didn't seem to mind.

"Look!" Toby slithered to the far right, where the gable end joined the sidewall. Here, a number of silver poles were jutting above the rake.

"What are they?" Frank asked.

"It's the scaffolding!" Toby told him. "This is how we get down." He made it to the edge and peered over. "Hmmm." The scaffolders had built platforms using planks, which was fortunate. The highest of these was merely inches from where he was standing. It would be an easy jump. A square gap allowed for a ladder to poke through. This would be the way down to the lower level. Toby could probably manage the ladder, and hopefully Frank could, too. Sal would find it easy. Hedda might have to succumb to a piggyback. What lay below, Toby had no idea.

"There aren't any hoomans, are there?" Sal whispered.

"Not that I can see. Not here, anyway. I suppose if they were still working this afternoon, the weather would have put them off," Toby surmised.

"It's putting me off, and I live outside," said Frank.

"Don't you have a nice warm burrow?" Hedda asked.

"I do," Frank said. "I don't spend much time there though. It's a bit lonely."

"You're welcome round at my log anytime," Hedda said and, when Sal gave her a questioning look, added, "That goes for all of you."

Sal relaxed. "Cor."

Toby had a feeling he might be seeing less of Sal from here on out. "Come on," he said. "Mind the gap."

He easily hopped over the six inches but, realising Sal would be unable to cope with the leap, stepped back and swept him up.

"Oof!" the rat grumbled. "So humiliating."

"I never say no to a lift," said Hedda. "Hedgehogs don't jump." Frank eyed her prickles—still, for the most part, protected by the corks—with some distrust. Toby returned once more. "Grab my collar," he said. Hedda was nimble enough on her feet that she could swing as Toby jumped. And she did so.

"Weeeee!" she sang.

"No creature left behind!" Toby grinned into the rain, his fur plastered against his skull. He couldn't remember the last time he'd been so wet. Maybe his memory wasn't as good as Clarissa's? She'd have told him exactly when that had last happened. Clarissa *always* kept receipts.

That left Frank, who easily cleared the gap too.

"One more obstacle," Toby called. "Then we'll be under some shelter."

"Pawesome!" Sal shivered with cold. "Let's get on with it!"

Sal conquered the ladder admirably. Perhaps knowing that he'd be able to take a break from the rain gave him the motivation, and he was down on the lower platform faster than a rat ... well, a rat down a drainpipe, really.

Hedda proved more problematic. In the end, Toby suggested she scootch into her protective ball and he would carry her down. It felt odd, having a hedgehog in his mouth, but she didn't seem to mind too much. Frank had to climb down under his own volition, and he did it in typical fox style. Head first. At the moment he lost his balance, he simply leapt onto the platform, landing softly beside Sal and making the poor rat jump.

Shivering but enjoying a breather, they shook themselves and rested, listening to the rain thundering on the wooden boards above their heads. The external wall of the manor was being repointed at this part, and the rendering had been chipped away to reveal the old bricks and the weaknesses between them. A crack, rather like a zig-zag lightning bolt, had split the walls asunder. "I'm amazed this place is still standing," said Sal, standing with his hands on his hips and inspecting the damage with the air of an expert surveyor. "I mean, I've seen some dicky old buildings in my time, but this one takes the biscuit."

"Don't mention biscuits." Toby was suddenly aware that he was hungry. What time was it? How long had they been struggling? It had to be dinnertime!

"Cracked like an egg," Sal continued, oblivious. "Held together with sticky tape and bad intentions."

Toby considered the crack more seriously. Sal hadn't meant what he said. He used the words innocently, in a light-hearted way, but this house oozed evil. There was no getting away from that fact. The rendering was a façade, something fake that contained the wickedness inside. Here, standing on this platform, the crack in the wall so evident, Toby shivered. What if the sour badness of Miranda Dervish was leaking out into the atmosphere?

What would that mean for Sun Valley?

"Are you alright?" Frank asked.

"Of course!" Toby shook himself again, spraying raindrops everywhere. "Let's head down to the bottom level. You go first, Sal."

"I'd love to," said Sal. "But I think we have a problem."

CHAPTER SEVENTEEN

"You're right. That *is* a bit of a problem."

Toby, fighting to keep his balance as a gust of wind rocked the platform, peered down the hole where the ladder should be. He could clearly *see* the ladder that should have been in the gap, but it had been placed on its side and secured to the bottom of the scaffolding with chains.

"Why have they taken the ladder away?" Sal squeaked. "What were they thinking?"

"I suppose it stops kids and trespassers climbing up when the workers aren't here," Toby suggested.

"And dogs, foxes, rats and hedgehogs," said Hedda. "Not that I make a habit of climbing ladders."

"Who does?" agreed Frank.

"Toby does," shouted Sal. He had to fight to make his voice heard above the rain and howling wind.

Toby poked at the hole with his paw, as though that would somehow replace the ladder or make the drop less steep. They were approximately fourteen feet above ground level. It would be too high to jump.

"If only we had parachutes," said Hedda.

"Are you serious?" Frank asked. "Absolutely not!"

"Nobody panic," said Toby. "We don't have parachutes, so we're not skydiving. And we don't have any rope, so even abseiling is out of the question."

"Halleluia," said Sal. "I think we already vetoed that idea."

Toby surveyed the platform. "We're not going to be getting to the ground that way, so we'll have to—" He hesitated. *Oh.* An opportunity presented itself, but this was the last thing he wanted to do. Reluctantly, he indicated the window to their left. Tall but only half as wide, it had multiple panes of glass, most of which had been individually boarded up, but not by the builders, and not recently. The majority of the square panes had been broken a long time ago, and now strips of wood and pieces of cardboard covered the holes.

"You want us to go through the window?" Sal asked, with the air of a rat about to rescind his best friend status.

"I don't want to go in there any more than you do —" Toby tried to say.

"Why? What's in there?" Frank was instantly suspicious.

"Nothing good, I'll warrant," said Hedda, although she didn't sound scared. More ... curious.

"You warrant right!" said Sal. "The last time we were in there—"

"Sal!" Toby cut him off. "We probably don't need to have this conversation right now."

"I don't know ..." Frank grimaced. "I'd like to hear it!"

Toby reined in his frustration. "Guys, guys, guys! What choice do we have? It's the window or a death drop!"

The animals regarded each other, blinking into the fierce wind. Toby was right. There was no alternative route.

"Just tell me honestly," Hedda said. "Is there anything in there that might want to eat us?"

What kind of barbarian would eat a hedgehog? Toby wondered. "No."

"But there *are* things that could hurt us," Frank pointed out. "We've already seen people arriving, and in my experience, it's hoomans who want to hurt us the most!"

"That's true, that!" Sal nodded vigorously.

"It is true," Toby agreed. "But we genuinely have no other way of getting down from here. I could probably levitate Sal and Hedda, but I can't do the same for myself or you, Frank. We're too heavy."

"Now there's an idea!" said Sal, clutching at the straw Toby had offered.

"Sal! We're not leaving Frank and Toby to make their way through this big scary house alone," said Hedda, utterly appalled.

Sal, seeing which way the wind was blowing—and boy, it was blowing so hard!—clamped his mouth shut.

"No creature left behind!" Hedda added, punching the air.

"Let's do it," said Frank.

Pushing through the window was the easy bit.

The cardboard had been sellotaped into place about a thousand years ago and the tape had become brittle. It had held on over the last few years thanks more to wishful thinking than anything else. The planks were nailed on over several of the broken panes, and these would not have budged easily, but there was plenty of space for Hedda and Sal to climb through, and even Frank was slinky enough that it didn't prove problematic. Toby went last and had to breathe in, but fortunately nobody mentioned the size of his belly or the generous nature of his furry rump.

Only now that they were indoors, away from the elements, did they realise exactly how wild it had been. The absence of the storm made Toby's head hum, and the lack of rain made his skin tingle beneath his fur.

They stood together, shivering and dripping wet, creating a puddle on the floor, staring down the long corridor before them. Before the point where this corridor joined the one opposite, beside the staircase, a couple of silver poles with a thick red rope had been put in place to create a temporary barrier.

Toby peered up. They were on the first floor, the one below where the Grim Brothers had lived in their equally grim bedsit while they undertook work for their mysterious employer. Toby hadn't had time to explore this floor at all when he'd last ventured inside the manor, but he remembered that the nursery was on the other side of the central staircase.

Ugh.

He was in no hurry to push that particular door open.

"It's horrid in here," said Hedda, curling her lip and scrutinising the old water stains on the ceiling and the bare bulbs swinging from filth-encrusted wires. Someone had been in here stripping the old wallpaper away, but much remained to be done. Although most of the remnants had been swept from the floor, the walls still exhibited several centuries' worth of décor, layer upon layer of odd styles. The top layer was a rather gruesome terracotta woodchip, but below that was one in mustard flock, and another in red silk. The bottom layer stood out the most: black and corrupt with black mould.

Toby swallowed. *Not nice. Who enjoys black wallpaper?*

He thought of Clarissa and her threats to paint the house red and black.

Witches, that's who.

"Let's go," he whispered. "Quietly." Without being asked, he hunkered down far enough that Sal could grab his collar and leap onto his back, but Sal chose to walk with Hedda instead. They made their way slowly along the corridor, past several doors. Toby averted his gaze from any that were ajar, catching glimpses of abandoned beds, piles of paint pots, upended dressing tables. This house could play tricks on you. If you looked too closely, it tried to suck you into its evil memories. He needed to maintain focus and get everyone else out to safety. What he did after that was on him, nobody else.

"It's coming on well!"

A man's voice boomed around the central staircase.

Toby froze. The others, trailing behind, followed suit.

Cocking his head, Toby listened. A woman's voice answered the man, the tone softer, the words indistinct.

"I should think it's costing an arm and a leg! A place like this," the man said.

Toby indicated the others should stay put. Frank nodded. Hedda and Sal instinctively drew closer to the fox. Toby left them, treading softly, pleased that his claws hadn't grown too much since his one and only visit to Pea a few weeks previously.

He became aware of movement in the stairwell

long before he reached the red dividing rope. Were the hoomans coming upstairs? He pressed himself against the wall, scarcely daring to breathe. He couldn't be caught here. Not with Hedda, Frank and Sal. That would spell disaster.

The woman said something about donations.

"From Lord Cryptid, you say?" The man with the deep voice sounded pretty peeved. "Well, Miranda, my darling, I'm sure Sooz and I would be delighted to match his donation."

Miranda? Toby almost squawked. *She* ***is*** *here!*

"This manor is a home for us all. A sanctuary from the crazy, unforgiving world outside!"

This guy had to be a lecturer. Or a politician. Or something. He liked the sound of his own voice, that was for sure. It echoed around the first floor and around the stairwell to the top floor too.

Miranda spoke again. Toby struggled to hear her, but he caught the words, "Too generous" and "Our mother will be most grateful."

Mother? Is this Miranda's brother? Is their mother still alive? Would that be the same woman I saw entering the nursery before?

Puzzled, Toby peeped out from his place overlooking the stairwell. The man—tall and somewhat portly, wearing a dark suit and with hair that might have been dyed—was staring at a giant painting hanging on the wall. It definitely hadn't been there the last time Toby had climbed these stairs. It depicted a beautiful woman in a garden with long, flowing hair, wearing a black dress heavily embroidered with symbols of some kind. She held an apple out to a bunch of cherubs who clamoured for her attention.

Toby recoiled from the image.

The beautiful woman's eyes shone with an unnatural silver light.

"We're so looking forward to the ceremony tomorrow," the man was saying.

"Indeed! Come," Miranda's voice summoned him away from the portrait. "Tea is being served in the parlour ..."

Her voice drifted away. The man took one more look at the portrait and followed the hostess, leaving the staircase empty.

Toby crept forwards and peeped through the spindles. The stairwell had been spruced up. Properly cleaned. The walls had been newly decorated. A sniff confirmed his observations. In fact, the downstairs had the distinctive whiff of new paint and wallpaper paste, new furnishings and new upholstery.

In so little time? Impressive.

He quietly retraced his steps. "Several hoomans downstairs," he warned his friends.

"Are we going to be able to get out without being seen?" Frank asked.

"It's risky," Toby admitted.

"I don't want to die!" Sal squeaked, a bit too loud.

"Ssssh!" Everyone else chorused at once.

Sal clamped his tiddly paws over his big mouth. "Hm um um um hmm!" he repeated.

"No-one's going to die," Toby hissed. *Not on my watch.* "There must be an alternative route out." *But if there is, I don't know of it.* "Would there be another set of stairs?" he wondered aloud. "A back staircase?" He'd seen those in historical dramas on the telly.

"Where would a back staircase be?" Hedda asked.

Toby resisted the urge to say, 'at the back', because it was a genuinely perceptive question. The central staircase was already at the back of the house, theoretically. But the back of the house often referred to the parts of the house guests wouldn't see, right? The scullery. The kitchen ...

That's right! The kitchen was on the lower level in the opposite wing. It stuck out from the rest of the house.

On his previous visit, he hadn't noticed any back stairs because he'd been focused solely on what a terrible ruin the place was. And he'd been distracted by the peculiar vision in the kitchen, as well as the barking dog.

"I think it's worth taking a look over there." Toby gestured at the corridor beyond the staircase. He knew the room at the very end was a nursery—he'd seen that in another of those disturbing visions—but he had an inkling it would be worth investigating what else lay in that direction.

"Are you sure we can't simply go down those stairs and make a run for it?" Frank asked.

"What's your top speed, bud?" Hedda asked him.

Frank shrugged. "I don't know. Thirty miles per hour, maybe?"

"Good for you. I can manage five."

"Five?" Frank choked. "Five miles *an hour*?"

Hedda glared at him. "Yeah. A human baby could outpace me."

"But—"

"And I can only run in short bursts!"

"Ah," said Frank.

"Yeah. So don't go thinking that I'm going to be outrunning anyone anytime soon. 'K?"

"Okay." Frank flashed Toby a bashful smile. "Back to plan B, I think."

"Right." Toby began leading them towards the staircase. "Shush," he reminded them, and they pitter-pattered over to the opposite corridor.

There had been changes here too. The wallpaper had been scraped away more thoroughly, down to the bare walls. Fresh plaster, still drying in places, had been layered in patches. The woodwork—on the skirting boards and the doors—had been sanded back and washed with sugar soap, ready for primer. The ceiling had been painted too, although it probably needed at least one more coat.

The first door immediately to their left stood ajar. Toby could smell a mixture of fresh scents as he passed. Fresh paint, wallpaper paste, new carpet, fresh cotton ... He wanted to resist peeking in, and yet his willpower collapsed and he paused at the door. He nudged it open.

The room had been decorated in white and cool grey. A huge bed with a carved headboard, covered in the squidgiest-looking bedding, took centre stage. Towels had been rolled neatly and arranged at the foot of the bed, with several fluffy wool cushions artfully placed against the pillows.

Toby held his breath, imagining that what he was

seeing would alter and his perception would morph into something ominous ...

But it didn't.

"Nice," said Hedda. "Although those cushions would be a nightmare with my prickles."

"I stayed in a hotel once," Toby said. "It didn't look anywhere near as lovely as this."

"She must have visitors," said Sal. "I wouldn't mind sleeping on that bed."

"You're not the kind of visitor that would be welcome," Toby reminded him.

Hedda giggled. "Nor me, I should imagine."

The image of a hooman finding Hedda in the foot of their bed one night tickled Toby. The humour warmed them all. They pressed on, with renewed energy, to the next bedroom. This time Toby had no hesitation in inspecting the interior. This room mirrored the first, right down to the arrangement of towels.

In fact, all six bedrooms on this corridor were virtually identical, bar a few minor details.

"Peculiar," said Toby.

"Maybe she's opening a hotel," Sal suggested, but that didn't ring true. Why would Miranda Dervish want to open a hotel?

Toby recalled the man with the deep voice

mentioning a ceremony. *What kind of ceremony? A wedding? Something else? What would it involve?* "I think she's having guests," he said. "Not many, but enough to fill these bedrooms."

"How many rooms are there downstairs?" Frank asked.

"Loads," said Toby. "Big ones and small ones."

They came to another door. This one was closed, and Toby had to stand on his hind legs and pull the handle. The door opened inwards, and as he tipped down onto his front paws, he spotted the steps.

This stairwell was cold. The steps were made of stone and had never been covered in marble, tiles, linoleum or carpet. They were worn in the middle from thousands and thousands of ascents and descents. The walls here were a mix of old, old bricks—red and uneven—and even older stone. If Toby wasn't much mistaken, this had to be part of the original house.

He leaned forward to peer down the stairwell. It was difficult to see because the steps curled tightly around themselves, but he could smell the tantalising rich aroma of roast beef.

Beside him, Frank noisily licked his lips. "Is this the way out, do we think?" he asked, sounding hopeful.

"I reckon so," Toby said. "The only problem is, if the stairs open directly into the kitchen and there are people inside, we're back to square one."

"One of us could nip down and have a look," suggested Hedda.

"I volunteer!" Frank said before anyone else could get a word in.

Toby chewed this over. "I'm not sure that's a good idea. A fox suddenly appearing in the kitchen would cause all kinds of mayhem."

"Hmpf," said Frank.

"It has to be Sal," said Hedda.

"Eh?" Sal took a step backwards. "Why does it *'ave* to be Sal? Maybe Sal doesn't want to go!"

Toby nodded. He grasped Hedda's thinking. "Because while hoomans hate rats in the kitchen—there are even songs about them—finding one under your French dresser isn't as far out as finding a fox foraging in your fridge or a hedgehog hoovering up the veggies in your vegetable rack."

"What about dogs?" Sal asked. "Everyone loves dogs."

"Not everyone, sadly," Toby said. "The Pointy Woman definitely doesn't. She's already tried to have me killed at least once!"

"It can't be Toby," Hedda decided. "It has to be you, Sal." She reached out to squeeze his paw.

He flushed. "Well ..."

"You're so brave." Hedda grinned.

Sal swallowed. "Okeydokey. I'll do it."

"Well done, Sal," Toby praised him. "Remember, quietly does it. We'll wait here for your return."

CHAPTER EIGHTEEN

Except Toby didn't wait. Not there at the top of the cold, draughty stairwell anyway. He left Frank and Hedda to keep an ear and an eye out for Sal and backed into the corridor.

The only room they hadn't peeped into on this side of the first floor was the nursery.

I don't want to, thought Toby, *and yet I feel compelled to. What a dichotomy! Who'd be a spell-bound hound?*

He studied the door. Closed. Freshly painted in white. It appeared innocuous enough.

It'll be another bedroom, thought Toby. *That's all. It's not as though The Pointy Woman is going to be bringing any babies back here, is it?*

And yet ... and yet ...

He balanced on his hind legs and placed a front paw on the handle. His skin reacted, his fur standing on end, a shiver running down his spine. The handle tilted as he pressed down. The door swung open.

He fell back, unwilling to cross the threshold. Not without seeing what lay inside first.

Not grey and white. Not like the other rooms.

The light in here was brightly dappled. Dust motes danced in the sunbeams. The light blinded Toby so much that he struggled to see.

There shouldn't be sunbeams, Toby thought. *It's raining. It'll be getting dark soon enough.*

A rectangular rug, as red as blood, covered the central portion of the floor. A crib made of dark, carved wood had been set upon the rug. It had been draped in a red gauze canopy. Besides the crib and the rug, there appeared to be no other furniture.

Toby became aware of a baby, not crying exactly, but making some sort of snuffling noise. He blinked rapidly, as though he could clear the bright, musty light himself and therefore improve visibility.

Come in, the room seemed to say. *Come in and play.*

Toby took a single step forward, his left front paw crossing over the threshold.

Welcome. Welcome. Soft voices ... Girlish laughter.

Play with us.

I'm imagining things, Toby decided.

"There, there." A voice to his left, this one definitely real. He snapped his head in that direction. A woman in a long black dress, the material shining. She stood with her back to him, gazing out of the window over the downs towards the sea. Her thick dark hair, arranged in complicated plaits and coils, had been piled on her head, giving her a strangely top-heavy appearance.

She half turned, and Toby could see that she was cocooning a baby in her arms, soothing it as it burbled gently to itself.

"Such a beautiful girl. Such a clever baby," the woman said. She had a heavy accent. Toby couldn't place it, but he would have guessed Eastern European. "Destined to become an adult who will dutifully serve her mama—"

***Serve** her mama? Such an odd thing to say,* thought Toby.

"Become as powerful as her mother. More powerful, perhaps ..." The woman rocked the baby, who responded by giggling in delight.

"If I only had one desire for you, my darling

daughter, it would be that the whole world became your plaything. A doll's house for you to do with as you wish."

Toby pulled a face. Most parents bought doll's houses for their kids to play with, they didn't seek world domination for them. *I don't like this vision,* Toby told himself. *I was wrong to open the door. I'm going to see how Sal's getting on.* He began to reverse.

"Wait, Toby," said the woman.

Toby froze.

She knew his name. This hadn't happened before when he'd entered any of the other rooms and experienced these odd flashbacks.

"Of *course* I know you, Toby. I know *all* about you." The woman, silhouetted against the window, turned a fraction more in his direction. He couldn't see her. Couldn't see the features on her face. He only knew that her voice sounded young. Younger than Miranda's. "I know that in years to come, unless you are stopped, you will thwart my daughter's endeavours."

Toby swallowed. *Does she mean this baby? What would I possibly do to a child? I would never hurt a child!*

"She won't be a child forever, Toby. She'll grow

big and strong." She held the baby out towards him so the sunlight played on her features. Pinched features. Eyes open wide. Dark and glistening. Uncanny.

Toby recoiled.

"What's the matter, Toby?" The woman's accent grew thicker with every syllable—*vot's da matter?* "Don't you want to greet your nemesis?"

"I don't—" Toby began to say, but the woman spun to face him, throwing the baby in his direction.

Toby howled and backed out of the room into the corridor. The door swung closed with a sharp bang. Something heavy clunked against it and dropped to the floor on the other side.

Toby, horrified, stood and stared at the bottom of the door, waiting for the baby to begin shrieking.

Silence.

Panting, his sides heaving, he lifted his head, eyes bulging. What had he seen? What had he seen?

Run, Toby! Run!

The girlish voices taunted him. He couldn't be sure whether he was hearing them or not. *Run!* They urged. *RUN!*

No longer entirely certain what was real and what was his mind playing tricks on him, he whined loudly and pivoted, throwing himself at the door that led to the back stairs and startling Frank and Hedda, who were directly behind it.

"What's happened?" Hedda asked, alarmed. "Your fur is standing on end!"

"We have to get out!" said Toby.

"Sal's not back," Frank said.

"Now!" roared Toby, pushing past them and almost tumbling down the stairs.

"Wait for me!" Hedda begged. She couldn't take the uneven steps as quickly as Frank and Toby.

Toby, still panting, his spine taut with loathing, battled his instinct and paused halfway. Hedda rolled into a ball so that Frank could gently nudge her down, step by step. Toby wiped at his mouth—he was drooling with fear—fighting to curb his impatience.

Sal picked that moment to appear. He paused on a step two below Toby, eyeing the others while wringing his paws together.

"What's up?" Frank asked, joining Toby on his step, Hedda in a ball at his feet.

"It's crawling with people down there," Sal reported. "There's loads of them." He glanced uncertainly between Toby and Frank. "There's a door at the bottom, but it's wedged open because there's access to a scullery and an old loo. I checked it out."

"Define loads," said Frank.

"Lots of people wearing white and black and going in and out of the kitchen. I dunno. Seven or eight, maybe." When Toby didn't comment, he added, "There's a whole new kitchen in there. Shiny appliances. It's big!"

For one awful moment, Toby thought he would faint. "It doesn't matter how many people there are," he managed, "we have to get out."

"There's a back door in the kitchen," Sal said. "That's open too because the hoomans keep going outside—"

That was all Toby needed to hear. "Get on," he told Sal, stepping down to get closer to him.

"But—"

"Get on, or I'll leave you here," Toby insisted through clenched teeth.

Sal swung onto Toby's back.

Without an instant's hesitation, Toby leaned over and clamped his jaws around Hedda.

"Ooooh!" she said, momentarily taken aback, and then Toby leapt down the remaining steps. The time for conversation was over.

"Eeeek!" Sal squeaked, barely keeping his grip.

Toby didn't hesitate. He dashed through the door and into the kitchen, rapidly taking stock of where he was. The back door, as Sal had said, had been wedged open.

A female voice shouted. Then, as Frank materialised, surprise turned to alarm and another woman shrieked.

Toby didn't care. He sped out of the back door and raced through the rain down the hill towards the lane. He didn't stop until he reached the gate, where he dropped Hedda—rather unceremoniously—onto the verge and allowed Sal to jump off.

Moving away from the others, he gagged and retched, thankful that the long grass hid him from his friends.

"Are you alright, champ?" Frank asked.

But Toby couldn't tell him what he'd seen. Wouldn't. In fact, he wasn't certain whether he'd ever be able to tell anyone.

Because as the woman in the nursery had turned towards him, as she'd thrown the baby at him and its swaddling had begun to unravel, he'd witnessed the impossible. Not a young woman at all, but an old woman, an ancient woman who had lived many lives over. Over and over. Her face was like parchment, her eyes shining with an unearthly light, the wrinkles so deeply entrenched that she might have been a concertina. And her hair? Coiled snakes, shifting in a mass, as poisonous as the blood that flowed through her veins.

Could that be Madame Minovska?

And could she be Miranda Dervish's mother?

CHAPTER NINETEEN

"Toby?"

The voice he needed to hear most in the world sounded oddly close. This had to be another one of those visions. He clamped his eyes closed, sinking into the sodden grass, needing a minute to get himself together.

"Toby? Are you hurt?"

It certainly sounded like Clarissa. Toby opened his eyes and gazed around. And there she was. Standing by the gate, dressed in black jeans, heavy boots and a stupid cropped denim jacket that would never keep her dry even in the lightest of showers.

"Clarissa?" Toby attempted to rise, his shaky legs refusing to work at first. "What are you doing here?"

"I could ask you the same."

He expected her to be angry, but her tone was laden with concern.

"Are you hurt?"

"No." Toby shivered.

Sal rushed towards Clarissa, diving between the slats of the gate to sit on her boot. "You wouldn't believe the afternoon we've had! Scary Mary!"

Clarissa, hearing the squeaking, peered down at her feet. Seeing Sal, she bent and scooped him up. "Let's go home," she said. "Come on, Toby."

Toby began to hurry towards the gate. Home sounded like the most pawesome place to be. On the sofa with a blanket, watching *Midsomer Murders* and nibbling crisp crumbs from Clarissa's lap.

Out of his peripheral vision, he spotted an orange flash. Frank had hidden in the bushes. He and Hedda were a long way from home too. Toby couldn't abandon them here.

He paused in front of the gate. "I have friends with me," he said. "We'll need to drop them off, if that's okay."

Clarissa nodded. "Alright," she said. "No problem."

He loved her for that. Her unquestioning acceptance.

"Are they all as wet as you?" she asked.

"Yes."

Clarissa jerked a thumb back down the lane. "I left the car at the bottom. I didn't want to get hemmed in by any other vehicles."

"Wise," said Toby. "There have been loads of comings and goings. Mostly comings, now that I think of it."

"Shall we?" Clarissa began to walk downhill, still cradling Sal.

Sal stretched his head above her shoulder so he could see Toby. "Nice an' warm up here, mate."

"We'll see you there," Toby told Clarissa, glaring at Sal. "One of our party is slower than the rest."

"Okay." Clarissa took off while Toby made his way over to Frank's hiding place.

"I've bagged a lift for us," he told Frank.

"With a hooman?" Frank grimaced. "I don't think—"

"You're a long way from West Hill," Toby reminded him. "And I know you could cover that ground easily enough, but Hedda can't."

Hedda poked her nose out of her own hiding place in a tuft of tangled bramble. Amazingly, most of her corks were still at the end of her prickles. "No creature left behind!"

"Exactly!" Toby stared pointedly into Frank's fiery eyes.

"If you're sure," said Frank.

"Clarissa would never hurt you."

Clarissa had been taken aback to find herself acting as a taxi for a fox and a hedgehog, but true to form, she didn't bat an eyelid.

"How did you know where we were?" Toby asked as they drove away from Blackwell Manor.

"I didn't," Clarissa said. "Not for certain. I ... had a feeling." She glanced in the rearview mirror at Frank, who was standing on the back seat, fighting to balance while panting like a steam train. "Is he okay?" she whispered.

"He's fine. He's never been in a car before."

"It's so fast!" said Frank.

"I know, right?" Sal, nestled in the folds of Clarissa's jacket, could only agree. "It does take some getting used to."

"You had a feeling?" Toby prompted Clarissa.

"Yes. I can't explain it. I was working—"

"As per—"

"I knew you were out. And then that storm

blew in, and something told me you were in grave danger. I couldn't shake the feeling. I decided to come and look for you—and the moment I jumped into the car, I knew *exactly* where you were."

"How remarkably witchy of you," said Toby.

"I thought so." Clarissa grinned. "So 'fess up, buddy. How did you get to Blackwell Manor?"

Toby stared pointedly out of the window. The sky, still heavy and grey, glowered down at them. "Probably better if you don't ask."

"Oh my." Clarissa breathed heavily. "That doesn't sound good. So, what did you think you were going to do while you were there?"

"I wanted to see if *she* was there."

"And was she?"

"She was."

Clarissa did a double take. Evidently she hadn't been expecting this response. "She *was*?"

"I told you she was living there. I could feel it. A bit like you knowing where I'd gone."

"Did you *see* her?" Clarissa needed to double-check.

Toby thought back to the moment near the barrier by the stairs. It had felt as though he was in her company and she had been merely feet away but no, he'd only *heard* her, not *seen* her. Unless ... Unless you counted the baby.

Had that been her?

"That place is evil," Toby said, which wasn't an answer to Clarissa's question.

"We're here." Clarissa pulled over on the side of the road, halfway down the hill from where Sparky and Old Pete lived. "Will this do?"

"It's perfect," Toby said, and Clarissa jumped out of the car and into the rain, Toby right on her tail, to open the back doors. Frank leapt out as soon as the door was wide enough and scrambled into the undergrowth, but Hedda, obviously, needed to be helped out and over onto the verge. Clarissa had a dog towel in the boot, which she used to transfer the hedgehog, setting her down gently, well away from the traffic.

"Thank you so much!" said Hedda.

"I'm terribly sorry about your balloon," said Toby.

"Oh, don't be." Hedda dismissed his apology. "I'll think of something else to do with my time, don't you fear."

"I'll come and see you soon!" Toby promised.

"So will I!" sang Sal, and Hedda beamed at her ratty friend.

"Can't wait!"

Toby, back in the car, wagged his tail in Frank's direction as Clarissa climbed in beside him. He wasn't sure whether Frank saw him or not, but he hoped so.

"Balloon?" Clarissa asked as she clipped herself in.

"Don't ask," said Toby. "You absolutely, genuinely, *totally* don't want to know."

Toby, basking in the warmth of his toasty, cosy living room, on the sofa and tucked under a blanket with Clarissa, sharing a bowl of popcorn with her—and Sal, of course—realised that his heart rate had almost returned to normal.

Perhaps Clarissa could sense that too, because as she handed him another piece of popcorn, she asked, "What scared you so much? It can't have been just *her*. I mean, you've seen her dozens of times."

Toby didn't want to think about what he'd seen. He didn't want Clarissa to know the details. He didn't want to scare her. And yet, pre-warned is pre-armed, right?

"I saw ... I think ..." He sighed. "I thought I saw

this Madame Minovska woman." That was as far as he was going. She didn't need to know any more.

Clarissa chuckled. "Well you can't have, babe. She's been dead a long, long time." Clarissa chewed on some popcorn. "Are you seeing ghosts now?"

"It didn't feel like she was a ghost," Toby told her. "I thought it was real at the time." He remembered her face, how it could almost have been carved from layers of dried parchment. The slow, deliberate movement of the coils piled on her head. He shuddered.

Clarissa felt the shudder and reached for the remote. Setting *Midsomer Murders* on pause—they'd seen this episode a dozen times—she reached down and caught Toby under the chin. "What aren't you telling me?"

"Nothing!" Toby protested.

"Madame Minovska is dead," Clarissa repeated. "Whatever you saw was one of those visions like you had before. That house seems to have a mind of its own. It'll be better for all concerned when it gets knocked down."

"Will it ever be knocked down?" Toby asked. "It's being refurbished super-fast!"

"What do you mean?" Clarissa asked. "They were only putting new windows in the other day."

"They must have builders in working around the clock, because from what I saw—" Toby indicated Sal, who had a paw in the popcorn bowl and was helping himself, his round cheeks stuffed like a hamster. "From what *we* saw, the whole of the ground floor and half of the first floor is already completed."

Clarissa screwed her face up. "You can't be serious. That would cost a king's ransom!"

"I'm totally serious! Brand new kitchen, brand new everything!"

"Lucky them." Clarissa pouted, probably thinking about her own lack of funds and the plans she had to revamp their kitchen.

Toby's ears pricked and he looked towards the window.

"What's the matter?" Clarissa asked.

"Someone's on the drive."

"At this time of the night?" Clarissa asked and set the snack bowl on the floor. "Maybe it's Ed." Throwing back the blanket, she looked down at her scruffy t-shirt, covered in bits of popcorn, and sloppy joggers. "Oh, crikey!"

"It's not Ed," said Toby. He would have recognised Ed's familiar tread. This was someone new.

Someone a bit ... slow and shuffly. "Would you like me to bark?"

"Not really," said Clarissa and reached for her slippers.

"They're going," Toby told her.

"Already?" Clarissa remained sitting on the sofa, unsure whether to go to the door or not. "Maybe they were at the wrong address."

Toby cocked his head, listening as a vehicle pulled away from the kerb outside. "Delivery," he said.

"Madness. You have to feel sorry for delivery drivers who are forced to work all hours of the day and night." Clarissa pushed herself off the sofa. "And in all weathers, too. It's horrible out there tonight!"

She headed for the door. Toby, on a whim, decided to follow her.

"It *is* a delivery!" Clarissa said, peering through the glass. "There's a box on the step. It can't be for me; I haven't ordered anything." She unlocked the door and took the chain off, pulling it open and stooping down. Toby stuck his head between her knee and her arm to get a better look. A sizable box with black writing on the side.

"It's light." Clarissa picked it up.

"Lazy Susan's Flowers," Toby read.

"Must be from Ed. I didn't know he was so romantic." Clarissa giggled and carried the box into the hall, setting it down on the floor.

Toby shivered. Clarissa hadn't closed the door. He squinted outside. A pair of eyes—shining green eyes—stared at him without blinking. Moriarty. She was sitting on the gatepost watching, even in the pouring rain, back hunched.

"Oh!" Clarissa's howl of revulsion diverted Toby's attention.

"Who would send this?" Clarissa cried, waving a card around. "What a sick thing to do!" She kicked the box away and the contents fell out.

A wreath of white lilies. Black bows. A funeral wreath!

Toby stared at the flowers, then at Clarissa. "Does it say who it's from?" he asked. "What's written on the card?"

"It says *Flowers for your funeral. Rest in Peace, Clarissa! A friend.*" She shuddered. "With a kiss. A single kiss!"

CHAPTER TWENTY

Toby had never seen DC Ed so cross.

Not-so-dead-to-me Ed had been a distressed Clarissa's first phone call, of course. Unfortunately, Ed had been pulling an extra night-shift, but he'd arrived at Chamberlain Drive as soon as he was able, shortly after eight this morning, famished and totally exhausted.

But not so exhausted that he wouldn't fight Clarissa's corner. Toby had to admire the detective for that. He was less impressed by Ed turning down Clarissa's offer of scrambled eggs on toast because Toby would have happily helped him polish that off. Sadly, it was not to be. After necking a mug of coffee in double-quick time—Clarissa claimed her boyfriend had a silicon-coated mouth, but Toby wasn't sure hoomans had silicon in their mouths—they had clipped Clarissa's lead to Toby and left the house to pay a quick visit to Lazy Susan's.

Clarissa had evidently forgotten about Toby's recent visit to the shop, so he had to cross his paws that the woman who worked there wouldn't remember him, otherwise he might end up in a whole heap of trouble.

For a change.

So here they were, Ed facing the employee across the counter, his face pale and his cheeks tense. Normally an agreeable and calm man, even Ed's knuckles were white as he fished his warrant card and ID out of his pocket.

Toby sniffed at the flower buckets nearby.

"DC Ed Plum, Devon and Cornwall police," Ed said. "I'm making some enquiries about a wreath that was sent to thirty-three Chamberlain Drive late last night."

"Oh." The woman twitched nervously. "Was there an issue with it?"

"Nothing wrong with the wreath," Ed snapped. Clarissa placed a hand on his arm. "Only the person who sent it."

The employee took a step away from the

counter. "I'm sorry. I can't control who orders our bouquets and wreaths. We only—"

"I need to know who sent it," Ed told her.

"I can't do that—"

Toby rolled his eyes and cocked his back leg, sprinkling the gypsophila and neighbouring ferns with some precious amber nectar.

"Yes you can," Ed replied, absolutely furious.

"Data—" the woman tried to say.

"If I have to get a warrant for this issue, believe me, I *will* do so, and then I will tear this place apart, stem by stem—"

"There's no need!" The employee was beginning to panic.

"And if you're hiding any financial discrepancies from the taxman, my people will find that out too!"

"I'll get the order book," the woman said, and hurried out the back.

Toby regarded Ed with more than a little admiration. Clarissa had been a jittery mess ever since receiving the wreath and hadn't slept a wink all night, but here was her secondary—Toby being primary—knight in shining armour to help her out.

The woman brought the book in and placed it on the counter so that Ed could see. "Thirty-three Chamberlain Drive, you said?"

"That's right." Ed squinted at the scrawl. "What does that say?"

The woman ran her finger across the entry. "Marie took this order right before closing last night. I'm surprised you had a delivery as we don't deliver anything after five as a rule."

"This was delivered a little before ten," Clarissa said.

"That's rather unusual," the woman said. "I'm going to need to speak to Marie about this."

"Or I can," said Ed. "You can give me her number."

The woman hesitated. Ed raised his eyebrows.

The woman swallowed. "Let me write down her number."

"Too kind," said Ed.

Back outside, Ed tried to call Marie. "Straight to voicemail," Ed grunted. "I'll try again in a bit."

Clarissa sighed. "Thanks, Ed."

"Don't be silly. What else do you expect me to do?" He threw an arm around her shoulders and gave her a hug.

"Shall we have a pootle around the park?" Toby suggested.

"I guess so," Clarissa agreed.

"Is there any chance we can go and have breakfast somewhere?" Ed asked. "My stomach thinks my throat's been cut!"

Toby gawped at Ed in alarm, but his throat appeared to be intact.

"You look as though you could do with something to eat too," Ed said, but unfortunately he was speaking to Clarissa, not Toby.

"There's a café along Mayflower Lane that serves lovely all-day breakfasts," Clarissa said. "But it's tiny and they don't allow dogs in."

Toby peered over at the crossing. He had a sense that he needed to be in the park. Right now. He weighed up the possibility of a sausage sammich—remote—versus a possible chat with Rory.

After Toby's experiences yesterday, it proved to be no contest. Rory won.

"Don't worry about me! I'll take myself across the road."

Clarissa glanced nervously at Ed. Ed looked from Clarissa to Toby. "Does he badly need to go or something?" he asked.

"Something," said Toby.

"He ... er ..." Clarissa was torn.

Ed huffed. "Come on then, we'll take him for a quickie."

"You can't come," Toby told him.

"What do you mean?" Clarissa asked him.

"In and out," Ed replied, assuming she was talking to him. "We'll hurry around the park and then go to the café. I'm starving!"

"Free, free, set me free," sang Toby.

"It's alright." Clarissa knelt and unclipped the lead.

Toby wagged his tail. "I'll come and find you!" he said and made a dash for the crossing.

Ed caught his breath. "What are you doing?"

"It's fine." Clarissa took his arm. "Trust me. You and I are going to have to have a chat one of these days."

"A chat?" Ed didn't sound as though he liked the idea of that. He stared after Toby, watching as the strange dog paused and waited for the lights to change.

"Come on." Clarissa tugged him towards Mayflower Lane. "A full English and a mahoosive pot of tea for two awaits!"

Toby had been right.

Rory was sitting waiting for him on a bench overlooking Swan Lake. He was nursing a cup of tea, only recently poured from his tartan-patterned thermos flask, judging by the steam drifting from it. He waved as Toby approached.

"Good morning, Toby!" He lifted the plastic cup in salute. "So glad you could make it."

"Did you summon me?" Toby asked.

"After a fashion. A little ring-a-ding-ding on the old mindwaves. It works a treat, and you are particularly susceptible to it."

"That makes me sound like I'm a weakling."

"Not at all." Rory harrumphed. "Perhaps it would be better to say you are *open* to telepathy."

"That happened to Clarissa yesterday," Toby said.

"It must be catching," said Rory, suddenly more interested in his tea than Toby.

"I can't stay long," Toby said. "Clarissa is only across the road having breakfast."

Rory nodded. "I'll get straight to the point then, Toby. It's my understanding that you visited Blackwell Manor yesterday." He framed this as fact, not as a question.

"Mmm." Toby was aware he'd been warned to stay away.

"I need you to tell me what you saw and heard."

"Everything?" That could take all day.

"Succinctly."

Toby had no idea what suck-sink-ly meant. It sounded like a job for a plumber rather than a spell-bound hound, but he jumped straight into what had happened, assuming Rory didn't need to hear the details of the hot air balloon jaunt.

"We ... er ... had to enter the house on the first floor, and we hadn't gone far when I heard *her*."

"The woman you know as Miranda Dervish?"

"That's right. I didn't see her, but I heard her."

"Who was she talking to?"

"Some guy. Smartly dressed. Older but not as old as you."

"Did you see his face?"

"Yes. Dark hair, neat beard and moustache." Toby thought back. "Thinking about it, I feel he may have dyed his hair and beard because it didn't fit his skin colour. Not that I know much about that kind of thing, but ..." Toby wobbled his head. "I don't think I paid much attention to that at the time."

"And you didn't hear Miranda mention his name?"

"No."

"Were *any* names mentioned?"

A light blinked on. "There were a couple. Sooz?"

"Sooz?" Rory grunted in satisfaction.

"I think she might have been related to the man on the stairs."

"Ah. That would have been Sir Thomas A'Delphi. Billionaire investor with strong connections to the Kremlin. His wife is Susannah Bartolph-Hoffs."

Neither name meant anything to Toby.

"Of course they'd be there." Rory sniffed. "Anyone else?"

"A Lord ... Cryptic. No. Krip ..."

"Cryptid?"

"Yes! Do you know him?"

"Oh yes." Rory nodded, his eyes serious. "Not a pleasant man at all. But then none of *her* followers are."

"Followers?" Toby's eyebrows performed a quick dance.

"What else did you hear?"

"Something about a ceremony," Toby said. "Tonight."

"Tonight?" This appeared to take the wind out of Rory's sails. He slumped, frowning.

"Yes."

"You're sure?" Rory poured his tea onto the grass beside the bench.

"Yes."

"So soon?" Rory said, more to himself than Toby. "We have to move fast—"

Toby gulped. "We?"

Rory stood and began packing his things away. "A figure of speech, lad. What I want you to do is go home and lock all your doors and windows—and don't answer them to *anyone*."

"But—"

"That's all you can do now. Find Clarissa and take her home."

"But there's something else," Toby said. Rory had started to walk away, or hobble might be a more accurate description. It wasn't hard for Toby to keep up.

"Go on," said Rory, although he didn't so much as pause.

"We went into the other wing and the bedrooms were newly restored. In the old nursery, I saw a woman."

"What woman?"

"A woman with a baby. She was dressed in a long black dress. All old-fashioned. Her face—" Toby shuddered.

Rory stopped. "Minovska."

"But she's dead," said Toby. Didn't Clarissa keep telling him that?

The old man began moving again, this time with greater haste, almost skipping as his bad leg dragged.

"Rory!" Toby ran to keep up.

"Go home, Toby!" Rory repeated. "Lock your doors!"

CHAPTER TWENTY-ONE

Toby, shivering a little, waited outside the café on Mayflower Lane, eliciting the sympathy of several passersby. Several of them stopped to pet him and told him he was a 'good boy'—which he already knew, of course—but he barely noticed them. He couldn't blame his feeling cold on the day's gloom because he recognised it for what it truly was.

Fear.

From where he was standing, he could see Sweet Pea's Parlour for Pampered Pooches, still closed up. No sign of Pea or Pickle, not in the shop or in the flat above. Toby wondered where they were and if they were okay. If it hadn't been for the pupnapping of Pickle's sister, he would never have known The

Pointy Woman was back in Sun Valley doing her thing.

Part of him wished he'd never found out, but, on the other hand, he knew without a doubt he would have to face her sooner or later.

He had no desire to place Clarissa in danger though. Rory had been intimating that this could be a possibility. Toby swivelled to peer impatiently through the glass door into the boutique café. Ed, looking profoundly fed up, was talking into his phone and patting his pockets. Clarissa was standing at the counter, laughing and chatting to the café owner. She looked better. Less pale. Breakfast had done her good. Ed had cheered her up.

Am I the one who brings her unhappiness? wondered Toby. *If I had heeded what Rory said and not visited Blackwell Manor yesterday, perhaps she wouldn't have received that awful wreath. If I didn't have the association with The Pointy Woman, Clarissa wouldn't even have needed to be involved. It's me who puts her in danger. Me who makes her unhappy!*

The realisation came like a stomach punch. *I'm bad for her. If I'm not with her, she'll be safe!*

He peered up and down Mayflower Lane. Where could he go? Perhaps in search of Pippin in the market. They could hide out together on the building site. There were no zombies left there anymore. Or he could run to the park and hide beneath a willow tree with the swans and the geese.

Hmmm. Maybe not ...

The market it would have to be. He began to head that way.

"Hey, Tobes!" Ed had come bustling out of the café holding a serviette aloft. "Come and see what I've saved for you."

Toby hesitated. It would be for the best to run and keep running—

Ed shot a look through the café's window. "Quick, you big dafty! Before Clarissa sees!"

His evident excitement to be sharing something with Toby and getting one over on Clarissa was irresistible. Toby abandoned his plan to run away and trotted towards Ed.

"You could show a touch more enthusiasm," Ed hissed and unrolled the paper serviette. "Sausage!"

Wow! A whole sossidge is a big deal for a little-ish dog. Toby wagged his tail gratefully. "You know what, Ed? I think I'm beginning to like you," Toby told him before giving him a paw and accepting the treat.

Ed crouched down beside him. "I've been called

back to work, Toby, so you need to look after Clarissa for me, alright?"

"It's the honour of my lifetime," Toby said, with his mouth full.

"What's he eating?" Clarissa asked, joining them in the street and pulling on her jacket.

"Nothing," said Toby and Ed together.

"Yeah, right." Clarissa elbowed Ed. "Don't encourage him. He'll put on weight."

"He'll never be overweight given the amount of running around he does! Like me!" Ed patted his stomach. "Back to work I go, and that'll probably be the best meal I have for the whole twenty-four hours!"

"I don't know how they can call you in when you only came off a shift five minutes ago," said Clarissa, sounding cross. "You ought to be getting some sleep!"

"Needs must. I'll only be there an hour or two, then I can go home and get some shut-eye."

"Before heading back to the station later!" Clarissa protested.

"Don't worry. I'm used to it." Ed leaned close to her and kissed her.

Toby pulled a face. "Ick."

"We have the whole weekend to do something

nice," he said. "Maybe have a day out in Cornwall with Toby or something."

"Sounds like a great idea!" Clarissa grinned. "What do you think, Toby?"

"I think a couple of weeks of duvet days might be better," Toby suggested, thinking of Rory's admonishment. There would be witches in Cornwall, exactly as there were in Devon. Clarissa needed to steer clear of them *all* until such time as The Pointy Woman had been removed as a threat.

Clarissa gawped at him. "Seriously?"

Ed grinned at her. "You two are so funny, talking away to each other."

"Haha!" said Clarissa and rubbed her forehead.

"Right! I'll leave you two to your stroll." Ed clapped his hands together. "I'd better go and collect my car. I'll ring you later." He hugged Clarissa once more, then winked at Toby and hurried off along Mayflower Lane.

"Shall we have a saunter around the park, Tobes?" Clarissa asked. "I need to work off my breakfast."

"I'd rather go home," said Toby.

"You would? Oh. We could have walked with Ed." Clarissa stroked his head. "Alright. I suppose I can work some of it off on the walk home."

"We should stop at the minimarket," Toby suggested.

"Good idea. I'm almost out of bread and milk. I might get some apples, too."

"Get enough snacks for a week of duvet days," Toby said as they began to walk towards the top of Mayflower Lane. "Cheese crisps for me. Kweesh for Sal."

"You can't be serious about duvet days!" Clarissa guffawed. "Not even you can watch that much TV. Besides, I have work to do!"

"As long as you're indoors, that's fine. You can do what you want. Better get some pizzas and chocolate—"

"You're not allowed chocolate."

"For you, not me!" They drew level with the minimarket. Toby stayed away from the door. He didn't want the proprietor to notice him. "Spaghetti hoops, vegetables and cheese. Maybe some bacon."

"This is turning into a long list. I didn't bring a shopping bag with me."

"You can buy them at the counter," Toby reminded her.

"Right." Clarissa shook her head, dropped the lead and began walking to the door. "You're a bit crazy this morning."

"Definitely get bacon," Toby called after her. "Enough for a week!"

"Goodness me," Clarissa grumbled.

"And fish fingers! And mayonnaise! I'm dying for a fish finger sammich!"

CHAPTER TWENTY-TWO

"Is the deadlock on?" Toby asked Clarissa for the umpteenth time.

"You know it is," murmured Clarissa.

"I think I'll check anyway." Toby padded out to the front door and, standing on his hind legs, verified that the chain was across and the deadlock was on. Once all four paws were back on the floor, he stood back and considered the door. The window beside the door didn't open. Neither did the peephole. But the letterbox did.

"*Super-glue*!" he muttered, waving a paw, and the letterbox gummed up.

There was no way that anything was going to be slithering through there any time soon.

Satisfied, he tippity-tapped across the wooden

floorboards and back into the living room. He'd pulled the curtains across the big window in here when they'd arrived home—heavily laden, much to Clarissa's consternation—from the morning's expedition, but Clarissa had insisted she wanted what little light the gloomy day allowed to filter in through the window.

Eventually, after a bit of a tug of war of viewpoints, they'd compromised on the curtains being half closed. Or half open. Depending on the way your world view works.

After that, he'd hurried out to the wizard shack in search of Sal. The rat hadn't been hard to find, curled tightly into a ball on his favourite cushion, dreaming about cheese.

Toby prodded Sal. "You have to come inside."

"Hyuh. Wha'?" Sal blinked. "Is it mornin' already?"

"What do you mean? It's lunchtime!"

"Already?" Sal sat up. "I ain't 'ad me brekkie yet."

"You'll have to have both at once." Toby indicated the door. "Come on."

"Into the house?" Sal queried. "In the middle of the day? Does the hooman know?"

"She won't mind. Will you hurry?"

"What's the bleedin' rush?" Sal grumbled, dragging his sorry bottom out of bed. "Is it rainin' again?"

"Just starting," said Toby. "Hurry."

Once Sal had finally shifted himself out of the wizard shack, Toby nudged the door closed and did something he rarely did. He reached out and magickly locked it. "*Fortress*!" he demanded, and the shack somehow manifested itself into something more solid than before.

"Something worrying you?"

Moriarty's voice, from above his head.

Toby experienced a pang of anxiety in the pit of his stomach.

"I don't know what you think I've done," Moriarty said. "But I haven't." She sounded hurt.

"To be honest—" Toby could hear a slight quiver in his voice. "I don't think you've done anything. I'm confused about a few things. That's all."

Moriarty gazed down at him with glowing—and knowing—green eyes.

"I'm sorry," said Toby. "I apologise for how I behaved."

"That's quite alright," said Moriarty. "We all go slightly nuts from time to time. I think it's something they mix in the pet food. Apology accepted."

They stared at each other a while longer. "Still friends?" Toby asked.

"Of course."

Toby hopped from one leg to another. "I need to go in. Keep an eye on Clarissa."

Moriarty nodded.

As he turned for the back door, she called out, "I saw who delivered your parcel last night."

"The florist?" Toby guessed.

"No. Some old man in a dark-coloured car."

That doesn't rule out many people, Toby thought. *Except women. And younger folk. People who don't drive. And people who drive light-coloured cars. Awesome.*

"I couldn't see his face, but he was a stiff old boy with a bad limp."

"You're sure? Wow." One person immediately jumped to the forefront of his mind. *Rory? Why would Rory try to scare Clarissa like that?* "Thanks," he said to Moriarty. "We'll catch up soon!"

Once inside the house, he bolted the back door and the dog flap before finally hustling Sal into the living room and onto the sofa.

"What about my lunch?" Sal demanded.

Clarissa peeled her attention away from her laptop. "Oh, Sal's here, is he?" she asked, pointedly.

Toby knew what she was thinking. She generally only allowed Sal in during the evening when she could keep an eye on him. He had a habit of eating anything that wasn't nailed down.

"Duvet day," Toby reminded her.

"You can't be watching the telly while I'm working! It's too distracting!"

"Come and watch it with us!" Toby suggested.

Clarissa sighed. "Sooooooo tempting, but no. I have three articles to finish and another one to begin researching ..."

"Maybe you could wear your headphones?" Toby said.

Clarissa glared at him. "Oi, cheeky."

"Just an idea."

Clarissa rummaged in her bottomless shoulder bag until she found her headphones. Popping them in, she poked her tongue out and returned her focus to the screen in front of her. Satisfied, Toby reached for the remote.

"What are we watching?" Sal asked, grabbing an edge of the blanket.

"There's some reruns of *Murder She Wrote*," said Toby. "Will that do?"

"Where's the snacks?"

Toby enjoyed Jessica Fletcher generally—perhaps not as much as Tom Barnaby—but variety is the spice of life. After two and a half episodes he realised he was finding it hard to stay awake, and so he began to doze.

Or he thought he was dozing.

He woke with a start to hear the rain spattering against the window. Out in the street, the cars driving past made that distinctive *shooshing* sound that tyres make when there's a lot of surface water. Lots of cars, he noticed. That meant commuters were returning home ... which suggested it was now dinnertime.

He jolted upright. The house was dreadfully quiet. No tippity-tapping on the laptop. No sizzling noises in the kitchen. No running water in the bathroom.

"Clarissa?" He jumped from the sofa and headed straight for the kitchen. Everything seemed neat and tidy in here. His water bowl had been recently filled with fresh water and there were fresh biscuits in his bowl—something Clarissa tended to do when she was going out. A snackette to tide him over.

Toby checked the back door. The bolt was in

place. The dog flap remained locked. Through the window he could see his wizard shack. The door was closed. Nothing out of place.

His stomach tensed with anxiety. He shot out of the kitchen and into the hall. The chain was off the front door. The deadlock had been undone.

"Noooooo!" he howled.

How had he been so deeply asleep that he hadn't heard her getting ready to go out? Had she gone to meet Ed? Had Ed phoned her? How had Toby missed a phone call?

Maybe she's popped out to see Mrs Crouch?

Yeah, that'll be it. That'll be it!

Toby wandered back into the living room. If Clarissa's laptop was here, that would prove she'd only nipped out.

It was!

But her handbag wasn't. And that was weird. She didn't ever take her handbag when she popped in to see Mrs Crouch ...

Toby climbed onto Clarissa's chair. Her laptop was open. He'd learned to use the keyboard and the mouse, and now he nudged the latter to get the screen to wake up and clicked through the windows to see what she'd been looking at before she left.

He hissed when he came upon a search for

Carnation Funeral Home, Prospect Place, Sun Valley.

What are you doing, Clarissa? You ***know*** *that place is bad news!*

Clarissa's email was slightly more enlightening. The last but one email had been sent to Clarissa at 15.36 by Rowena Gubbens, her boss at *The Celestine Times*. Toby clicked on it and read:

Clarissa,

Regarding the article you're writing for us on haunted funeral homes, I had some interesting information from Madam Redd. Remember her? I'm sure you were on her podcast recently, weren't you? Anyway, she claims that there's a funeral home close to you that's haunted. It's too good an opportunity to miss.

I've arranged for Ali Broccoli, one of the freelance photographers we use down in your neck of the woods, to meet you there at 5.15. Let me know how you get on?

Rowena

Toby re-read the email. It could be genuine. Of course it could.

But it wasn't. There was something wrong ... He scanned the email again, becoming increasingly panicky. *Breathe*! he told himself. *Breathe*!

Then he spotted it. The email address was wrong. It hadn't come from Rowenajgubbens@celestinetimes.co.uk. It had been sent by Rowenajgubbens@celastinetimes.co.uk. Toby couldn't imagine that a newspaper as globally renowned as *The Celestine Times* would spell its own name incorrectly!

Sal yawned noisily and slithered off the couch, the blanket slipping to the floor. "Boy. I'm starvin'. I could eat a scabby horse! Hey!" He fluttered a piece of paper around in Toby's direction. "Is this for you? It's got hooman writing on it."

Toby jumped down from the table and joined Sal.

"What does it say?" Sal asked.

"Hey Tobes! I didn't want to disturb either of you. You looked so cute. You must be tired. I need to nip out but don't think I'll be long. We'll have bacon for tea! See you later! Clarissa. Kiss kiss kiss." Toby howled. "Didn't want to disturb me? What was she thinking?"

Sal backed away. "What? You don't want bacon? It's cool. We'll ask her for cheese!"

"I have to go after her!" said Toby.

"She's a grown lady. Ladies don't like to be

chased too much, y'know? Ya gotta play a little hard to get. Nice boys never win. Hey!"

Toby was already running for the front door.

"Where ya goin'?"

"After Clarissa," Toby called back. "Stay here and don't answer the door to anyone!"

"As if I'm gonna." Sal sounded confused. "It's not as though I can reach to answer the blo—"

But he was talking to himself.

Toby had gone.

CHAPTER TWENTY-THREE

Clarissa had taken the car. Toby paused long enough to stare at the space where it had been. She hadn't been gone long. Part of the asphalt where it had been parked was still dry, although the rain was valiantly working on that.

No time to waste. Toby pressed on, running along Chamberlain Drive—no sign of Mason and his siblings, given the weather, or Mrs Crouch in her garden. Once out of Chamberlain Drive, he had to navigate a busier road. Buses, cars and trucks thundered along this one, showering unwary pedestrians and magickal dogs alike with puddle water. Toby, quickly sodden, blinked water out of his eyes and pressed on. In a few more minutes he was on the pavement in front of the minimarket, the park ahead on his left. A quick right turn down Mayflower Lane, all the canopies pulled in and the businesses—with the exception of Goober's the Chemist, which was still open—closed for the day. Even the market had packed away and the council had been out and cleaned up. The burger van was operating, but there was no sign of Pippin.

Shame, because Toby dearly wished for some backup.

A left from the market and then a quick right brought him to the pavement opposite Prospect Place. He waited a moment while a battered white van accelerated out of the cul-de-sac towards the junction and turned left in front of him, its tyres squealing. Crossing the road, he stood at the top of the street, gazing along it. The garage, several buildings down, was open. He could hear spanners clanking and the sound of a hammer beating away at something, and tinny music from a radio.

Clarissa's car, a foot away from the kerb, had been parked at the bottom of the road, close to the funeral home.

Toby's heart leapt. If the car was still there, everything was probably alright. He was worrying over nothing. Breathing somewhat easier, he set out at a quick trot, ignoring the startled look of the mechanic who came out of the garage as he passed and nearly tripped headlong over him.

He stopped briefly alongside Clarissa's car. The engine was warm, and steam sizzled from the bonnet as the rain pelted it. The windows were steamed up too, as though Clarissa had sat in there waiting for Ali Broccoli to arrive. But evidently this Ali—or whoever—*had* made it because Clarissa wasn't in the car now. Toby, on his hind legs, peered into the driver's side. Her car keys weren't in the ignition and her bag had gone.

Okay.

He surveyed the Carnation Funeral Home with dread. It hadn't changed in the slightest since his previous visit. Still as filthy and rundown as ever. The windows encrusted with muck and dust, the double wooden garage doors crumbling into sawdust. One of these stood ajar.

Reluctantly, Toby made his way to it and poked his head around. Ears pricked, he listened.

From somewhere to the right and above came the sound of movement. Footsteps. In the living or office accommodation above the garage.

Thank goodness.

Clarissa must be exploring the upstairs with the photographer. *Won't she be surprised to see me?*

Toby's relief made him lightheaded. He moved further into the garage, skirting the old funeral car still covered in its protective sheet, the tyres as flat as dabs. He was about to call out and let her know he was here and could she give him a ride home and would she please not ever go out anywhere without letting him know in future ...?

Except as he opened his mouth to bark, he heard a voice. A man's voice. The footsteps were coming down some creaky stairs now. No carpet. His voice echoed. Toby waited, not wanting to disturb Clarissa if she were engaged in conversation.

"Yep," said the voice. "Worked a treat. She's on her way to you now. Mm-hmm. No. The dog wasn't with her."

The hackles on Toby's neck stiffened. What was this? What was the man saying? He could only be referring to Toby, and that meant he was speaking about Clarissa too. *On her way to you? What does that mean? Why hasn't Clarissa taken our car?*

The man stepped inside the office. Youngish. Thirty or so. Sandy hair, shaggy like you'd see on a surfer. "I'm going to lock up now and make my way back."

Toby crouched beside the hearse, trying to avoid being seen. As he did so, something underneath the car glinted and caught his eye. He stole a quick look. Then a longer look. *Is that a mobile phone?*

As if by magick, the screensaver appeared and the phone began to ring. Toby jumped.

"What's that?"

Eek! The ringing had alerted the surfer dude. Toby was about to take to his heels when he realised he recognised the caller's name. *Ed! That's Clarissa's phone!* He snaked forward on his belly, grabbed the phone in his mouth and extracted himself with difficulty.

"There you are!" The surfer dude was reaching down to grab his collar.

Ugh! Blasted collars! More trouble than they're worth!

Toby recoiled and dodged and evaded the guy's grasp, pivoted and darted for the open garage door. He was through it and halfway along the street before his would-be captor could finish cursing him.

I need to hide. Fast.

The nearest opportunity was the garage, so Toby threw himself inside.

"Hey, buddy!" A young mechanic smiled down at him. "You okay?"

Toby cowered away from him. Who could he trust? *No-one.*

"Awww!" The mechanic held out a hand, inviting a sniff. "It's alright. You're safe. Did someone hurt you?"

Toby slipped away behind a jacked-up car, then further back into the garage behind an enormous plastic tub of something called Swarfega, which was an interesting shade of green and had a wonderful smell. Behind him, he could see a back door. With any luck, that would open into an alleyway and he could escape through there.

"Bless!" said the young mechanic, advancing on him. "Poor thing. I hate it when people are cruel to animals! It's so backward!"

An older man sauntered towards them, wiping his hands on an oily rag and shaking his head. "Like you, Hayden. Bloody soft in the head you are!"

"Maybe." Hayden laughed. "Better to be soft in the head than an animal abuser."

"Amen to that," the older man said. "See if you can grab him, then. We don't want him getting hurt in here."

"Have you seen my dog?" The surfer dude was at the entrance, peering in.

Toby peeped out from behind the tub.

"You've lost your dog?" Hayden asked, straightening up and walking towards the newcomer. "What breed is he?"

"Erm ... a bit of everything," the surfer dude said. "He's yay-high." He patted his knee.

"What's he called?" Hayden asked.

"Why all the questions, mate?" the surfer dude asked. "Either you've seen him or you haven't."

"Sure, but I mean, he might have come in here and we haven't seen him. There are so many hiding places. Give him a shout," Hayden suggested.

Toby appraised Hayden positively. *Wily*, he noted. *A friend to the underdog.*

The surfer dude stood where he was, his eyes burning. Suddenly, he turned on his heel and stormed away.

"Whew. Bad vibes." Hayden whistled long and low. "I know a weirdo when I see one."

"He sure was," the older mechanic agreed. "But if that *is* his dog, we probably should have given him back."

"There's no way that dog belongs to him," Hayden said. "If he did, he would have come out when he heard his master's voice. Am I right?" He walked slowly towards Toby. "Hey, boy! What are you carrying in your mouth?" he asked.

Toby stepped out from behind the Swarfega and

wagged his tail as a thank you, then dashed out the back.

"Hey!" Hayden yelled, but Toby was already sprinting towards the marketplace.

And *nobody* was catching him until Clarissa was safe and sound.

CHAPTER TWENTY-FOUR

Sun Valley's police station was a peculiar mix of the old and the new. The building itself probably dated from sometime towards the end of the nineteenth century, but it had been added to over the past decade or so, with a new reception and accessible ramp, sliding glass doors and a sophisticated intercom and security system.

That made it tricky for a schnauzer-collie-whippet-terrier-thingie to gain access under their own steam. Toby, Clarissa's phone clamped firmly in his mouth, had to wait for some unsuspecting hooman to let him in.

It was just his luck that there wasn't much going on in Sun Valley this evening. Perhaps the weather dissuaded folk from coming out and about and nicking things or generally behaving like idiots. And maybe it was a bit early in the evening for burglaries. What did Toby know? He sheltered under a tree and waited, trembling with anxiety.

Come on, come on, come on.

At last, somebody arrived in a silver Mondeo and jumped out. A young woman with ramrod straight black hair and skin-tight three-quarter-length jeans teamed with an oversize flumpy puffa jacket. She stalked towards the doors and pressed the button. Toby hurried out from his shelter and along the ramp. The woman spoke to a voice on the intercom and stared at the camera above the door, making a V for Victory sign and poking her tongue out. The door buzzed and slid open. Toby hurried through at the same time as the woman.

Now, how to get Ed's attention?

The woman hastened to the reception counter and banged on the glass. "Wakey, wakey!" she called and, when nobody immediately answered her, tutted and rapped on the wall. To Toby's left was a seating area where people could wait to be seen. It had been furnished with dark blue armless chairs, a water cooler and a waste-paper basket, along with a vending machine that served drinks. Directly opposite this was a door with a sign that said *Private.*

Authorised Personnel Only. Toby knew from old that beyond that door were interview rooms and offices.

Given that Ed could be classed as authorised personnel, Toby understood that if he could get through that door, he would probably be able to track Ed down by smell.

Assuming Ed was even in the police station to start with and not at home tucked under a blanket with Netflix and a mug of Horlicks.

"Yo!" The woman banged on the glass again. "Hurry up!"

Toby considered the private door. It had one of those systems whereby you swipe your ID card and it lets you enter. He'd never worked magick on an electronic system before. He hazarded a guess that if he blew the electrics—which would be relatively easy with an incinerate spell or something similar—this might backfire. What if he permanently locked the door? That wouldn't get him where he needed to be.

But it did give him an idea.

What if he caused a fire? Just a baby one. An itsy bitsy one.

Everyone knows that if a fire alarm sounds, *everyone* is required to vacate a building. That would mean Ed would have to come outside and it would be much easier to talk to him.

But a *fire*?

Playing with fire is always a risk. Toby tipped his head back to study the ceiling. Definitely sprinklers.

"Yo! Yo! Yo!" The woman had started to slam the glass with her open palm. Time was of the essence.

Toby set Clarissa's phone gently down. Without getting too close to the bin in the seating area, he imagined a spark among the discarded paper cups and general detritus. "*Ignatio*," he muttered. He waited a moment, not entirely convinced much had happened. The problem was, the inside of the bin was probably damp, given that people threw away their water and hot drink cups there. He'd have to add a pinch of mental—not *actual*—gasoline to his spell. "*Ignatio*!" he said, with a touch more fervour.

The young woman glanced over her shoulder at him. "Do you work here?" she asked Toby, and laughed like a drain.

Toby ignored her. The bin had started to emit strange noises. Crackles. A hiss. As he watched, smoke puffed out. *Here we go*.

He scooped up Clarissa's phone and moved to the exit. Waiting.

It didn't take long. The sensors were top of the

range and, within moments, the smoke alarm in the reception area had begun its insistent shriek. Instantly, the sliding doors opened. Toby heard the sound of chairs scraping and the thudding of feet. Voices asking questions or shouting orders. The clink of keys.

The 'private' door opened, and an older officer dressed in a black t-shirt and black cargo pants hurried out, a number of civilians behind him. The wiser among them had remembered to bring their coats, jackets or umbrellas.

There was a *whoosh!* from the seating area and Toby turned his head. *Oopsie.* The bin was well alight, and a column of fire had started climbing the wall.

"Everyone out, please!" the first officer called, motioning to the woman by reception.

"I need to see someone!" she said.

"Well, that's not happening now, love. In case you haven't noticed, the station is on fire!"

"That's not my fault, is it?" the woman bellowed.

"Can you come out into the car park?" the officer asked.

"Not until I've spoken to someone!"

Toby watched as more pairs of legs hurried past him. *Come on, Ed. Where are you?* More officers in uniform, then several wearing suits. Ed would be in a suit. *Is that him? No. That one?* There! *At last.*

Ed hurried out of the station and down the ramp without spotting Toby, so Toby sprinted after him.

Workers were mustering at the far end of the car park, but Toby didn't let Ed get that far. He threw himself under Ed's smartly shining shoes, almost tripping the poor detective up.

"What the—" Ed recovered himself without faceplanting the asphalt. "Toby?"

Toby dropped Clarissa's phone on Ed's foot. "I need your help," he said.

"Are you shivering?" Ed knelt down, stroking Toby's back. "Are you cold, mate?" He reached for Clarissa's phone. "What's this?" He squeezed the button on the side so that the screen came alive. A close-up of Toby's face lit the screen. "Is this Clarissa's phone?"

"Are you going to ask any more spectacularly stupid questions, Ed?" Toby asked. "Yes, I'm shivering. No, I'm not cold. Yes, that's Clarissa's phone. Obviously. I. Need. Your. Help!"

"You seem agitated." Ed glanced over to where his colleagues were grouping. "I wish you could tell me what's wrong."

"I *can* tell you what's wrong. The problem is not

me. It's *you*!" Toby barked in frustration. "If only there was a spell ... If only I could make *you* spellbound!"

Ed frowned at Clarissa's phone. His eyes clouded. "Has something happened to Clarissa?"

"Yes!" Toby barked.

Ed regarded Toby more thoughtfully. "It has? Bark once for yes. Twice for no. Has something happened to Clarissa?"

"Yes!" One bark.

"Has she had an accident?"

"No!" Two barks.

"Is she at home?"

"No!" Two barks.

Ed shifted uneasily. "Is she in danger?"

"Yes!"

"Is she with anyone?"

"Yes!"

"Someone she shouldn't be?"

"Yes."

"Oh, blimey." Ed fiddled with Clarissa's phone. "Where?"

Toby gave Ed his best hound-dog look. *How am I supposed to answer that?*

"Sorry. Sorry." Ed shook his head. "Yes. No. Yes. No. Erm ..."

Behind them, glass shattered. Ed cast a worried glance back at the station. The reception area was well alight. In the distance, they could hear the sound of sirens. The fire brigade were on their way.

Ed reconsidered his last question. "Do you know where she is?"

Toby thought for a moment. He didn't know for certain, but yes, he had an idea. "Yes!" One bark.

"Okay. Okay." Ed stood and slipped Clarissa's phone into his pocket. "Let me go and chat to my boss and I'll be right back."

Toby hurried over to Ed's car to wait. The sky was lit up red and blue, the station glowing yellow. The crackle of flames sounded stupidly loud. *I didn't mean to burn the place to the ground,* thought Toby, worrying about the young woman who'd refused to leave reception. Gazing about, however, he spotted her at the far end of the car park with everyone else, still ranting about how no-one wanted to deal with her complaint and now she wanted to lodge a new complaint about how she was being treated and ... and ...

As the first fire engine turned into the car park, Ed sprinted back to his car. He opened the passenger door for Toby and then jumped into the driver's side. Buckling up, his breathing had become ragged.

"How bad is it, Toby?" he asked, but of course, Toby couldn't give a yes or no answer to that.

"I don't know," said Toby, "but probably not good."

Ed took a breath, straightened his shoulders and turned on the ignition. "Okay. I'm going to look a right idiot if you're barking randomly and this whole thing is in my head, but here's what we're going to do. As I drive, I'm going to ask left or right. You bark once for left, twice for right. Maybe three times for straight on, in case we come to a crossroads or a roundabout."

"And what if you go completely wrong, Ed?" Toby asked.

Ed pressed his lips together and frowned. "You do talk to Clarissa, don't you? And she understands you."

One bark.

"Wow!" Ed massaged his forehead.

"Deal with it later, Ed!" Toby said. "Let's get going."

"You're right." Ed surmised from the urgency of Toby's bark exactly what the dog was hinting at. "Okay. Left or right out of the car park?"

CHAPTER TWENTY-FIVE

"I think you should stop here," said Toby.

It had taken them longer to get to Blackwell Manor than it normally would have, but that was because Ed had trouble following barked instructions. Either that or he didn't know his left from his right.

"It's dark out here," said Ed, peering through the windscreen at the winding black tarmac on the narrow road ahead of them but not slowing down. They hadn't worked out the number of barks required for stop.

Toby clamped his jaw around Ed's wrist.

"Ow!"

That did the trick. Ed jammed the brakes on.

Toby waved a paw at the passenger door and

pushed it open, jumping out into a puddle at the side of the dark road. *Ewww!*

"Where are you going?" Ed called.

"You missed the turn, you muppet!" Toby dodged out of sight. He had to get Ed out of the car somehow.

Ed manoeuvred the car, reversing back a short distance—cautiously because the passenger door was still partially open. He found a wider part of the road and carefully parked before jumping out and reaching into the back seat for a heavy coat and a torch. Switching the torch on, he walked around the car to close the passenger door and lock up.

Toby, satisfied Ed was going to follow him, emerged from the nearby bushes.

"Sorry about your shoes, Ed."

The bottom of Ed's smart suit trousers and his polished Brogues were already thick with slimy mud. No doubt he'd regret not wearing something more substantial soon enough.

"It's pitch black out here," Ed complained again. "Why would Clarissa be here?"

Toby led him back the way they'd driven, to the turning Ed had missed. Toby didn't blame him for not seeing it. There was no signpost here. Nothing to suggest that the road—actually little more than a track—went anywhere important.

"This way," said Toby, beginning the trot up the hill.

Ed followed him. "You seem to know where you're going," Ed said, but doubtfully. "I'm still not entirely convinced ..." He paused, his eyes trained on something at the top of the hill. "I thought I saw a light for a moment. Is there a house here?"

Toby barked. "Yes!"

"Alright." Ed redoubled his efforts, puffing as the incline increased. It was easy to forget how steep the start of this hill was, and how long the lane was if you had to walk it. They kept on, even Toby beginning to labour, until eventually the track levelled out and they found themselves at the gate.

Ed reached for his phone. "I wonder if I can get the coordinates," he mumbled, but after a minute or so of faffing around with it, he shook the phone—as though that would help—and threw in the towel. "No signal." He spent a few seconds examining the keypad to the right of the gate, but the code was hardly going to magick itself into his brain and so, again, he admitted defeat and climbed over. Toby squeezed through the struts.

Whining quietly, he hunkered down. Ed knelt beside him.

"What?" Ed asked.

Toby whined again, softly, then crept forward in a crouched position.

"Are you saying to keep quiet?" Ed whispered.

Toby whined softly, once.

"And stay out of sight?"

Again, Toby favoured him with a gentle sound.

Ed breathed deeply. "Alright." He turned off his torch and they huddled together, waiting for Ed's eyesight to become accustomed to the darkness. When he was set, he squeezed Toby's shoulder and the pair of them walked on, Ed keeping close to the verge and staying in the shadows.

As they rounded the final bend, two things became apparent. The manor was sparkling like a Christmas tree, and The Pointy Woman had lots of visitors. There were vehicles—mostly smart, virtually new cars with a healthy number of larger four-by-fours—parked outside the barn and lining the drive, but from the point where the track finished and only a winding path remained, lights had been carefully placed en route to the entrance of the manor. As they drew closer, Toby realised these lights were fat pillar candles placed inside glass lanterns. The light they threw didn't go far, but they were effective in making sure you didn't stray onto the grass or into a puddle.

Ed sank behind the last car before the lights began, and Toby joined him. "What's going on here?" Ed muttered and took out his phone again. "Still no signal," he grumbled, and then, quick as a flash, snapped photos of several of the number plates of the vehicles surrounding them. "Must be some kind of party."

Silhouettes moved behind the windows.

"Toby?" Ed smoothed Toby's head. "Are you certain Clarissa is here?"

Toby made the soft whining noise.

"And she's not attending the party?"

Two short whines.

"That's a stupid question, maybe. Why would she be attending a party at such short notice? I mean, I suppose she could be, but she didn't say anything about it this morning." Ed mulled things over. Eventually, he whispered, "Is this related in some way to that wreath she received?"

Toby couldn't know for certain, but it seemed likely. He whined his response.

"I managed to speak to Marie, and she claimed some old guy came in and ordered it late yesterday, right as she was closing up. She said she wouldn't be able to deliver it until this morning, so he took one they had on display and said he'd drop it off himself."

Headlights came into view behind them, the vehicle's tyres spitting loose stones. Ed scrambled to the side of the car he and Toby were hiding behind so they wouldn't be seen. They crouched, waiting as the car located a parking space—with difficulty—and a pair of figures stepped out and made their way towards the path.

"It's going to be so good to get together again," said a female voice. "I've missed these ceremonies."

"It looks like a good turnout, too," replied a gruff male voice.

"I find myself yearning for the circle. For the call of the dark!"

"Let's hope they've secured a worthy sacrifice," the man said. "It's not the same when they resort to goats."

Toby gagged. *What? They're sacrificing goats?*

The couple pulled level with them. They were both wearing long, dark cloaks with hoods and, when the woman angled her face to speak to the man, Toby spotted the shining white of a mask.

"It's been so long. I'm certain that Miranda will have pulled out all the stops!" The woman laughed, a delicate sound that turned Toby's blood cold for some reason. "I expect she'll have a few surprises in store."

The voices faded away as the pair made their way along the path.

Ed's breath whistled in his chest. Toby, close to his knee, felt him quiver.

"Did you hear what they said?" Ed whispered. "They were talking about sacrifices!"

"I heard," said Toby.

"What a bunch of weirdos." Ed squeezed his mobile once more. "Come on, come on. Give me a signal. There are too many people here. I'm going to need some backup!" He surveyed the screen, held the phone up, moved around with it. "For crying out—"

"We have to go in!" Toby interrupted him.

Whether Ed had understood Toby's urgency was difficult to tell, but he edged around the car. "I need to get in there."

"*We* need to get in there," Toby repeated.

"I don't have reasonable cause ..." Ed muttered. "But if Clarissa is in there ..."

"I don't know where else she'd be," Toby told him.

"I'll look like a right idiot if she isn't."

"She is."

"But if she's in danger ..." Ed stood, and, for one horrible moment, Toby had a feeling the DC was going to head straight for the front door and ask for Clarissa. The Pointy Woman would laugh in his face then knock him down with one tap of a sharply pointed fingernail.

Toby jumped at Ed and grabbed his sleeve, yanking him back to safety.

"What?" Ed asked, shaking himself free. "You don't think I should go in?"

"Not alone. Not through the front door," Toby told him. "If you insist on going inside, I'll have to show you the back way."

CHAPTER TWENTY-SIX

"This is ridiculous," moaned Ed. "I'm a police officer! I have a warrant card!"

Toby rolled his eyes. He'd brought Ed around the back to the broken coal bunker door. He'd been afraid that The Pointy Woman or Madame Minovska or somebody would have replaced it, but no, the cellar remained open to the elements. Seemingly most of the recent remedial work had taken place at the front of the manor where it was most obvious, and the rear had been neglected. All fur coat and no knickers, Mrs Crouch would have said.

Together, Toby and Ed had walked past the lean-to, which was still in the same decaying condition. The most noticeable difference at the back of the building was the amount of light illuminating the surrounds, originating from the windows and door of the new kitchen. People in chef's whites and young men and women in black trousers and white shirts were shuffling around inside, but because they were all so busy, Toby and Ed had managed to sneak past without anyone seeing.

Thankfully.

Ed took a long look at the back door as if considering whether they should try their luck by going through the kitchen.

"Ed," Toby explained in his most patient voice. "Either you're doing this legally or you aren't. You can't walk straight in, either at the front *or* at the back. If you want to find out what's going on without The Pointy Woman stabbing you with her toxic claw, then you absolutely *have* to take a more surreptitious route."

Ed turned to frown at Toby. All he'd heard was a long series of woo-woo-woo-ruh-ruh-roo-roo-woos. "Clarissa is going to have to give me lessons in speaking dog, I reckon." He sighed. "I take it we're going down here."

"Roo!"

"Heaven help me. Okay." Ed stuck his head through and then followed it with the arm holding his mobile phone. "It's pitch black down here!" His voice echoed. "Must be a long way down." He leaned further. "I can't see how far." That was good enough for Toby. He barged into Ed's rump as hard as he could. Ed squawked and tumbled forward. He landed on the coal pile and slithered safely down to the floor, pieces of coal tumbling after him.

"Ow!"

"Soz," said Toby. "It wasn't that far though, was it? Catch me!" He jumped into the hole.

"Crikey, Toby!" Ed groaned as he picked himself up. "I think I've broken half a dozen ribs!"

"You exaggerate!" said Toby, shaking himself off.

"I've dropped my mobile." Ed crouched down and patted the floor, sending coal scattering in all directions. Unable to find it, he took out his torch and switched it on, cupping the beam to reduce the amount of light thrown. "There it is." He grabbed the phone and quickly swung the beam around the cellar, spotting the door. "Carefully does it," he said, and switched the torch off. "Ugh. It smells old and damp down here."

Ed turned out to be good at creeping. Maybe it was something they taught at detective school. He also had a lot of patience. More than Toby, in fact. Whenever they neared a new door or a turning, Ed would pause and listen. At the point at which Toby would have made a move, Ed would drop his hand in front of Toby's snout as if to tell him to wait.

A glimmer of light led them to a flight of stairs. Ed pocketed his torch. On the landing above, the lights were on. Toby recognised this as the corridor from the other day. The kitchen was through one of the doors at the top. A cloakroom or something through another.

Ed put a finger to his lips and they climbed the steps, pausing at the top. Through the door came the sounds of a busy party. The clink of glasses. Laughter. Chatter. People moving around. Somewhere there was a piano playing.

In the light, Ed looked a right state. He'd torn his coat *and* his suit trousers at the knee, plus his hands and face were covered in coal dust. Toby nudged him, directing him to the cloakroom. Ed held the door open and they entered together, locking it behind them. The cloakroom was old. The sink was a robust, ceramic affair with heavy, gilded taps, the toilet a mighty beast with a big yawing mouth and a wooden seat. The cistern was one of those built above your head, with an iron chain pull, making the most of gravity.

And it was cold.

Ed was staring at the hooks behind the door.

Several garments hung limply from them. Cloaks! Pulling off his coat, Ed quickly washed his hands and face, then yanked at a cloak. Dust bloomed in the air. It smelt fusty.

But it would do.

"How do I look?" Ed asked.

"Like a detective playing dress-up. Is there one in my size?" asked Toby.

"What are we going to do with you?" Ed asked. "Maybe you could stay here?"

"Not happening," Toby retorted.

"Or ..." Ed swung about, the cloak whirling around, sprinkling another cloud of dust. "See how voluminous this thing is?"

"I like your thinking." Toby dived under the folds of the cloak and huddled against Ed's legs.

"Just don't trip me up, okay?" Ed took one more look in the mirror. "I don't have a mask," he said, pulling the hood lower over his face. "We'd better stay where it's dark."

Fortunately for Ed, this wasn't as difficult to do as he'd first thought. With the exception of the kitchen, which blazed with light, the rest of the manor had been lit by lamps and even flaming torches in several places.

"Health and safety?" Ed muttered. "*What* is going on here?"

He edged out into the long hallway, the one leading to the main staircase and the entrance, Toby clamped against the side of his right leg, surveying the partygoers as best as he could without exposing his face. Almost everyone was wearing some kind of face covering. Most preferred the anonymous porcelain disguise, but a few had more elaborate coverings, including veils or scarves.

Opposite them, the dining room had been laid out with an opulent spread. The sort of thing that wouldn't have looked out of place in a Victorian period drama. The long table had been piled high with what Sal would have called 'delectables'. Platters containing meats or cheeses. The odd fancy kweesh. Pies and pastries. Salads. A whole pig. Roasted chickens.

Ed took a swift tour of the dining room. "No crisps," he muttered. "No cheese and pineapple on sticks. What kind of a buffet is this?"

"You don't have a drink, sir!" some blustering buffoon called out to Ed, and quick as a flash, a young waitress handed him a glass. Ed tipped his head carefully away, thanking her and raising his glass to the chap who'd called him out, then angled himself towards the pig and away from those who peered his way, glittering eyes curious behind their masks.

"Smells good," said Toby, although he wouldn't have been able to eat a mouthful, so sick to the stomach was he.

"Speaking of smells," Ed whispered, "can you smell Clarissa?"

"Not yet."

"Wait a minute, wait a minute," Ed hissed. One advantage of finding themselves in the dining room rapidly became apparent. Those who did want to eat had to lift their masks or remove them altogether. Ed snaked out a hand and grabbed a stray face covering from the dining table while its owner grappled with some green grapes. Prize in hand, they swiftly exited the dining room. Dodging into the room opposite, Toby glued to his side, Ed found what would probably become a library once it had been fully fitted out. For now, the room contained shelves, some comfortable chairs and an old desk, but not much else. Ed hurried to cover his face with the mask and rearrange his hood.

"That's better," he whispered to Toby. "I feel more incognito now."

"You should have taken a moment to clean your

shoes, I reckon," said Toby, and did his best to rub the muck off with his rump.

"What are you doing?" Ed asked, moving back into the hallway with great difficulty. There was every danger he'd trip over Toby and give them both away.

"What are we doing, you mean?" A petite figure gliding past him stopped. "We'll be going through to the ceremony room shortly," she said, her eyes sparkling with amusement through the holes in her mask. "Have we met?"

Toby peered out of the gap in Ed's cloak. She didn't smell familiar. *No, you haven't met*, Toby telegraphed.

"Who can tell?" Ed replied, in what Toby assumed was his flirty manner. It was pretty cringeworthy.

"In that case, if you're free after the ceremony ..." She leaned in towards him and lifted her cloak to display lacy stockings ... but also exposing the bottom half of a sharp knife tucked into a blood-red leather sheath.

Ed forced a laugh. "I'll certainly look out for you." His voice seemed higher in pitch than normal, Toby thought.

The woman slunk away.

"Crikey," Ed moaned. "What was she planning to do with that knife? Let's find Clarissa and get out of here."

"That's the idea, Ed!" Toby said.

"Sshhhhh!"

"Sorry, yeah. Shhhh!"

They strolled in the direction of the piano room and stood for a while, observing the partygoers. Ed scanned for clues as to who these people might be, wishing he'd taken photos of more number plates. For all he knew, these folk were blameless innocents, nothing to do with Clarissa's sudden disappearance, but the weirdness of the situation meant he was taking no chances. The front door was standing open, allowing people to come and go at will—probably to get some air or to take a cigarette or cigar break—and Ed, growing tired of fruitless people-watching, stepped outside. Reaching for his phone once more, he lifted it towards the dark sky—but before he could so much as check the signal, one of the hospitality staff appeared at his elbow, standing so close to Ed he almost stepped on Toby's paw.

Watch it, buster! Toby glared at the newcomer through the folds of the cloak.

This staff member, an older man wearing a brocade waistcoat, had a definite, although undefinable and yet somehow malevolent, presence. He smiled tightly at Ed and held out a gloved hand. "Sir, as you'll recall from your invitation, the use of electronic devices is strictly forbidden this evening. I'm certain you won't mind if I take this from you."

Ed hesitated.

"Sir?" The man cocked his head, the smile fixed, his eyes hard.

Collecting himself, Ed placed the phone into the man's hand. "Of course. My mistake."

The man bowed. "If I were you, I'd go inside, sir. The weather is most inclement and the ceremony is about to start."

With that, the heavy vibration of a gong filled the air. At once, everyone stopped what they were doing and fell silent.

"As if on cue, sir." The man dipped his head once more and indicated the hallway. "After you."

The shimmer of the sound of the gong seemed to last an eternity. Even before it faded away, the gong was struck again. From there it began a slow but rhythmic pounding, the echo rolling around, probably reaching into the far corners of the entire manor.

Toby pressed against Ed as he stepped inside the hall. From beneath the cloak, Toby had a good vantage for watching people's feet. The other party-goers drifted along the hallway, all heading in the same direction. They moved slowly, almost gracefully, and Toby noticed that nobody carried their drinks or food with them. Ed joined them in what rapidly became a procession of dark cloaks, many with heads bent, moving in time to the slow beating of the gong.

Toby kept pace with Ed, his snout busily sniffing the scents of fresh paint and varnish, noting the newly decorated skirting boards and the restoration of the polished marble floor, but he couldn't find the slightest hint of Clarissa. Towards the end of the hallway on the left were double doors. These had been thrown open to allow easy access.

As Ed and Toby entered the room, Toby almost forgot to hide, so entranced was he. He hadn't explored this room on any previous visit. It was a good size! Easily the biggest in the manor. Like a small ballroom, perhaps? The illumination was muted, utilising an odd mix of contemporary and older lighting. New-fangled directional lanterns—the kind you'd find in theatres—shared space with ridiculously dated, lit torches, as though the interior designer hadn't been able to decide between medieval castle or jazzy nightclub. In addition, tall candles on iron brackets spat and hissed. Smoke curled towards the ceiling, pooled there, and then dropped, creating a smog-like atmosphere. Three walls had been painted red and black, and heavy black curtains hung over the windows. The floor was red too—or perhaps it was being lit in such a way that it appeared red.

The fourth wall—the external wall—had scaffolding against it. If you peered closely through the hazy gloom, you could pick out where the plaster had fallen away, as well as the cracks in the old structure.

Towards the front of the room was a raised dais with access from all sides. This had been decorated with silver sigils and arcane symbols that sparkled in the light. Toby recognised some, although not all, of them. He shuddered.

"I don't like this, Ed." Toby trod on Ed's foot to get his attention, then sneezed. The place stank of heavy incense.

"Sssh!" Ed hissed.

Despite the pervasive air of excitement, the congregation—because this is what they had evidently become—folded into position without speaking or jostling each other, forming an incomplete circle. Ed, unsure where he should stand, took a space to one side close to the door and waited to be reprimanded or directed elsewhere, but no-one blinked an eye.

The gong finally stopped beating.

The doors were closed.

All electric illumination faded away.

Silence.

There was the softest of tings. As though someone had struck a tiny triangle.

Toby slipped out from beneath Ed's cloak and crept towards the right-hand side of the room into the deep shadow beneath the scaffolding. He wanted to skirt his way right around the room and investigate the various smells. He didn't think he'd be able to approach the dais without being seen, but—

Ting!

This time the sound was louder.

Ting!

And louder again.

Toby remained where he was, crouching as low to the floor as he could in case the lights suddenly all came on at once.

One of the curtains was pulled aside, exposing an open door. Three people stepped through and into the room, two wearing black cloaks and one, the shorter and slimmer of the three, in a cloak as deep and red as freshly spilt blood. There was a sudden explosion of sound. Applause. Whooping. Whistling. The red-cloaked figure climbed onto the dais and raised her arms in greeting. She wore a mask, much the same as everyone else's, except hers had a bright red mouth.

"Friends! Friends!" she called in an effort to calm the reaction.

Toby's hair bristled. He recognised that voice. *The Pointy Woman!*

"Friends!" She laughed, her grating tone a slap in the face to poor Toby. "Please. Thank you. Thank you!" She clapped her hands lightly and offered an almost inconsequential bow.

"Welcome!" she sang. "Welcome to our first gathering in Blackwell Manor for nearly thirty years!"

Another rapturous round of applause.

"Mainly thanks to the generosity of your donations, we have been able to begin restoration. We anticipate the entire manor will be habitable within six months."

More cheering.

Toby curled his lip.

"To celebrate our reformation and renaissance, tonight we will honour the dark gods—with not one but two sacrifices!"

The congregation roared. Only Ed stood mute, silently watching events unfold. Toby pressed himself back against the wall, feeling old plaster crumble behind him. Ed cast a seemingly casual glance over his shoulder. Two cloaked figures stood on either side of the double doors.

"I'd like to introduce the first of these sacrifices to you now." Miranda made a tiny gesture, and the pair of cloaked figures who'd accompanied her into the room made their way towards the rapt spectators, reaching for their first victim.

"Someone who invited themselves along but would have been far wiser to have kept their distance." Miranda threw her head back and cackled. When she'd finished, her eyes swept the congregation, licking her lips in anticipation. "My lords and ladies of darkness, please welcome ... Detective Constable Ed Plum!"

"What?" Ed scrambled backwards, but the cheering, gloating circle closed in on him. Greedy hands ripped at his cloak and mask and tossed them aside.

Ed lashed out. Generally he could handle himself but, seriously outnumbered, on this occasion he was easily subdued. Still, he threw out—and managed to land—a few punches before one of the heavier guards smashed their fist into the side of his skull.

Ed slumped to the floor.

Toby recoiled in horror.

Uh-oh, he thought. *Now we're in deep doggy-doo-doo!*

CHAPTER TWENTY-SEVEN

Ed, only semi-aware of what was going on, was hauled towards the dais and forced onto his knees before it.

"Peace," called Miranda, and the hubbub of excited voices, fuelled by adrenaline and bloodlust, abated. "Let us behave with the decorum that a celebration such as ours requires."

Many in the congregation dipped their heads.

"Bring the other in," Miranda ordered, flicking a finger towards the door through which she'd entered. The curtain was drawn back once more, and Toby's heart sank. He watched in horror as Clarissa, hands and legs bound, was bundled through. She struggled but was no match for the behemoths manhandling her. They forced her down to kneel beside Ed, facing the salivating throng.

Clarissa! Toby shouted, but only in his mind. *I'll save you! I'll find a way!*

But how? What magick did he know that could possibly help in this situation? How could he free both Clarissa and Ed? How could he fight off all the guards and the cloaked men and women? What could one unassuming schnauzer-collie-whippet-terrier-thingie do?

If he'd been able to get outside, perhaps he could have called on all of his friends to join him here and help storm the building. Frank and his woodland mates. Pippin and her stray friends. Moriarty and her fellow felines. Unfortunately, he had no chance of gathering everyone in place quickly enough. Plus, there was the teeny-weeny matter of escaping from this room without being apprehended.

Attracting Miranda's attention would do him no favours.

They're not actually going to sacrifice Clarissa and Ed, are they? Toby asked himself. But looking around at the other masked faces, reading their body language, the fervent gripping of fists, he decided this would be the most likely outcome.

I have to stop it! But how? I'm on my own,

thought Toby. *What should someone so humble and powerless do in this situation? What would the books suggest I do? What would Old Joe think to do?*

For a minute, Toby couldn't think straight. The Pointy Woman's shrill voice hurt his brain and clouded his thought process. She trilled on, showing off to her admirers and donors. He shook himself, clearing his head.

FOCUS!

Focus!

Focus ...

Small actions ... Small actions ...

"And without further ado, I want to introduce you to the woman you're all *dying* to meet!" Miranda Dervish tittered at her own joke. "My lords and ladies, let me bring out the one for whom all this has been organised. The one who guides us in the ways of darkness. The one we live to serve. My mother. *Our* mother!"

The side door opened once more and the room, already quiet, became still and heavy with expectation. An ancient woman stepped through the door. No mask here. Her dead eyes, peering out of a wizened face the colour and texture of dried-out parchment, raked the congregation, the lips parted in a semblance of a smile but actually more of a disdainful sneer.

"Welcome, Madame Minovska!" Miranda curtseyed deeply.

"Welcome!" the congregation echoed.

The old woman joined her daughter on stage, shadowed by two burly figures, arms out and palms up, carefully carrying ...

Toby blinked. *Yoikes*! Long swords!

The pair took their places in front of the dais, heads down. They manoeuvred the swords in swift, easy movements, swinging them down until the tips rested against their toes.

Minovska turned to face the congregation. "I am not one for ceremonies," she announced in her heavy accent. "I value no gods or demons other than the Lord of Darkness himself. I am wedded to him as he is to me. I serve him and him alone. I have no need of any of you, and I care not whether you remain or leave."

Miranda shifted nervously. "Mother—"

"Blood magick is the only magick of any importance. Blood magick ensures all my aspirations are fulfilled. I harbour no emotional connection to any of you, and I desire none—"

"Mother ..."

Madame Minovska turned a withering glare in Miranda's direction. "Listen to my snivelling wretch of a daughter. Her power is petty, much as she is. Once, I had high hopes for all she would achieve, yet she has failed me as everyone eventually does."

The audience, suddenly uncomfortable, began to react. There were some whispers. A few people shifted further from the dais.

"I am as old as time. I have lived a million lives and I will live a million more. The blood that is spilled here tonight will ensure this is the case." She gazed around the room, her eyes beginning to shine with a supernatural, silver light.

Toby held his breath. If he didn't breathe, if he made himself as minute as possible, then surely she wouldn't see him ...

One idle thought bounced into his brain. *She won't see me at all if I shut off the lights!*

Small deeds.

"Let the bloodletting commence," Minovska said, parting her mouth in some sort of rigor mortis grin.

Her companions, the men with the swords, raised their heads, eyes shining as bright as Madame Minovska's. Miranda stumbled away from them. "Mother?"

The swordsmen lifted their weapons.

A woman in the audience swooned.

Toby imagined the candles in his mind. "*Extinguish*!" He spoke the word aloud, maximising the intent. As he did so, Miranda's head whipped round in his direction.

Every candle in the room sputtered out.

Blades whirred.

Someone cried out. A cry that was caught horribly short.

Liquid spattered against the floor and walls.

Pandemonium erupted. Cloaked figures began to push towards the double doors. Toby, his eyes rapidly adjusting to the darkness, was relieved that he'd hidden in the shelter of the scaffolding. It protected him from the crush.

People were screaming orders. Women were crying.

Toby ignored them all, turning his attention to the figures kneeling before the dais. Ed and Clarissa. They were both there. Both intact. Unlike some poor unsuspecting soul who'd been standing too close to the swordsman on the left.

Madame Minovska, eyes blazing, spat instructions. "Kill them all!" she rasped. "Every last one of them. Tonight I will bathe in their blood and see in the dawn in the company of my master!"

"If you're killing everyone, start with him!" Miranda bellowed and, to his absolute horror, Toby realised she was pointing directly at him in his hiding place under the scaffolding.

"No, don't start with me. I'm really little," he said. "I don't have much of the magick master-summoning liquor inside me!" He slid backwards against the wall, putting distance between himself and Minovska's henchmen.

"I knew you'd be here, you blasted runt!" Miranda made her way down from the dais as the swordsman advanced on Toby.

Toby reversed into the corner. *Nowhere to go from here,* he thought. The swordsman leaned towards him. Toby focused on the shiny tip. "*Gelata*!" he ordered and, as his would-be killer reached in to deliver a final blow, the sword wobbled.

Confused, the swordsman pulled the weapon back. It flopped in his hand like a stringy strip of liquorice.

Toby danced away, winding through the legs of those in the congregation still struggling to get through the doors. Delighted with how his spell had worked, and intent on jellifying the other sword too, he hurried to the far side of the room as Miranda struggled to find him, crouching down to see where he'd disappeared to.

"Kill them all!" Minovska bellowed, her eyes shooting fire. While Clarissa strained at her bindings, tears streaming down her cheeks, the remaining swordsman took his place beside Ed. He lifted the sword high and began to swing. Toby, unable to get a clear view, thanks to people pushing and shoving around him, had to dart out into the open, but even as he opened his mouth to utter his spell, The Pointy Woman grabbed him by the neck and forced his face into the floor.

Toby squealed and wriggled, frantically striving to free himself. The sword began its downward loop. The Pointy Woman's nails dug into Toby's flesh.

All seemed lost until the air began to crackle with a strange energy. A low hum started to build, filling the room and becoming louder with every passing second until the air itself started to vibrate. A mist rose from the floor. The swordsman had stopped mid-swing, confused by the change in atmosphere. The Pointy Woman loosened her grip. Toby, almost choking, slid free of her.

Minovska held out her arms. "Master?" she asked. "Did I do enough?"

But it wasn't her master. Thirteen figures rose from the mist. Thirteen apparitions, each garbed in clothing from a different place and time. A druid. A washerwoman. A soldier from the Crimea. A warrior from the African plains. A voodoo priestess. A man in simple hose and shirt. A woman in a sari, a thick plait falling below her waist. A wizard in sparkling blue robes, clutching a staff. A wizard dressed all in black. A young girl in shorts and a pink t-shirt gripping a plush rabbit to her chin. A tall man in furs. A monkey. And an old man with a pronounced limp.

Rory?

Toby gawped. *What?* Fearful of what was about to occur, he threw himself towards Clarissa. He crouched in front of her as though his limited mass could prevent harm befalling her.

"Minovska!" Rory called. "It's over. Come with us."

The old woman turned to face Rory, her lips pulled back in revulsion. "Come with you and face infinity locked away from all I hold dear? Never!" she growled.

"You hold nothing dear," the druid said. "Except your own immortality."

Minovska sneered. "You and I have nothing to talk about, Aeron. Begone."

"We don't leave without you. Not today," said the washerwoman, her tone mild and yet fearless.

"None of you has a right to lay a finger on me!" Minovska spat. "You are no better than me, no matter what you pretend. Not you, Aeron. Not you, Bethsheba, no matter your airs and graces." She turned to Rory. "And certainly not you, Ruaidhrí, my treacherous lover."

"There is good and evil in us all," the wizard in black admitted. "But there are limits."

"There are *no* limits!" Minovska hissed. "Not for the truly powerful." She jerked a clawed finger towards her swordsman. "Why are you standing there? Kill them!"

"Mother! No—" The Pointy Woman rushed towards the dais, almost directly at Clarissa. Toby didn't even think. He bolted out to meet her. Her foot met his stomach. He briefly recalled how she had kicked her bag in front of Old Joe and caused him to trip, and now ... in a twist of fate he couldn't have foreseen, it was she who misjudged her own footing, tripping on Toby ... and it was she who was falling ...

Straight onto the henchman's sword.

Her eyes bugged.

The swordsman ripped the weapon free from her writhing body.

She collapsed onto the floor. Twitched once. Became still.

The thirteen figures began a slow advance on the dais. The henchman hefted his sword once more, but the wizard in blue smashed his staff onto the floor with such power that the room shuddered and the swordsman cowered away, dropping his weapon and holding out a hand in a plea to be spared.

Not so, Minovska.

"You'll never take me alive!" she hissed and, as the thirteen figures reached for their magick with which to bind her, she sucked in a noisy breath and began to shrink. Smaller and smaller. Ever smaller. And the smaller she became, the more rapidly she shrank, until she was a pinprick of silvery light virtually indistinguishable from the other markings on the dais.

And then she was gone—and the thirteen figures had disappeared with her, sinking back into the mist with barely a whisper.

Only the two swordsmen remained, and a few shell-shocked partygoers. Clarissa moaned. Toby hurried to find a way to loosed her bindings, averting his gaze from The Pointy Woman. "Unravel," he muttered. "Loosen!"

Blasted knots!

But, once Clarissa and Ed had been freed, and Clarissa was helping Ed out of the room, Toby paused for a moment and inspected his adversary. Properly inspected her. Sniffing her all over.

And yes.

Dead.

Justice had been served.

The Pointy Woman would never bother him or Clarissa again.

EPILOGUE

"Surely if someone falls on their sword, it means they die with honour?" Godfrey the goose nodded around at all his fellow goosey mates, seeking approval for his clever observation. There were a number of honks and a few hisses. Whether they were in agreement or not was anybody's guess.

Toby, sitting on a stone slab under an enormous weeping willow tree on the banks of Swan Lake, puffed out his cheeks. He'd arrived here at dusk with the express intention of keeping his promise to the geese to read them a bedtime story and send them off to sleep. He'd been here for over two hours, he'd missed dinner, he'd recited as many fairy stories as he could remember off the top of his head, and all he'd achieved so far was an empty tummy, a dry throat and a cold bottom.

Part of the problem was that Godfrey, the goose who'd been giving Toby so much grief, was an argumentative troublemaker who would, quite frankly, have benefited from a kick in the pants. Having failed to send anyone to sleep with *Little Red Riding Hood*—geese weren't afraid of wolves, apparently; and *Cinderella*—Godfrey was rooting for the stepsisters; and *Sleeping Beauty*—Beauty was too fussy and needed taking down a peg or two—Toby had recited his own recent adventures instead.

Most of the geese—there were about sixteen or so; they kept arriving and departing like planes at Heathrow's Terminal Four, so it was difficult to keep track of them—had been held rapt by the story, even applauding whenever Toby described using his magick. He exaggerated his successes, of course. All in the name of a good story.

But not Godfrey. Oh no. Godfrey wanted to second guess and twist everything. Here he was, championing The Pointy Woman and properly ruffling Toby's feathers. Or fur. Or whatever.

"She didn't fall on her *own* sword," he told Godfrey, not even hiding the ice in his tone, "she fell on someone else's sword!"

"Ouch!" One of the older geese shook his feathers. "Christmas dinner."

Christmas came early for me, thought Toby. *I'm pleased to be free of her.*

"I like the bit in the balloon! Toby the Intrepid!" said a gosling and yawned.

Yawns, as you know, are magickal activities. One yawn can spread like wildfire. They're catching. In this case, *finally*, the geese began to look snuffly and sleepy and dopey-eyed. *Why didn't I think of that?* Toby wondered. *I could have sprinkled a snoozy spell ages ago and I'd have been home in time for pasta and wine. Or ... maybe not the wine. Ed and Clarissa will be seeing to that, no doubt.* They'd spent a great deal of time wrapped in a blanket in front of the television over the past few days, getting over their encounter with Madame Minovska.

I ***knew*** *we'd need enough supplies for a couple of weeks of duvet days*, Toby thought triumphantly. It gave him enormous satisfaction to be right.

Again.

"That's it from me," said Toby, pushing himself off the stone slab with difficulty. His bones were stiff with cold. There was a proper bite in the wind tonight. Never mind autumn. It felt as though winter had arrived early.

"Going so soon?" Godfrey enquired.

"I ... er ... yes."

Godfrey nodded around at all the other geese, and a few ducks that had snuck in round the edges of the group to listen. "All that remains for us to do is thank our guest in our usual fashion. Let's give it up for Mr Toby Spellbound!"

Toby hated the expression 'give it up'. What was he supposed to give up? Biscuits? Not going to happen. Nonetheless, he wagged his tail as the geese honked and the ducks quacked and a couple of coots grunted.

"It's Toby Silverwind," he mentioned to Godfrey as the noise subsided. "I *am* spellbound, but my name is Silverwind."

"I see. Good, good, good!" Godfrey began to hustle Toby out from under the willow tree. "Hope to see you again soon! Bye!"

Away from the shelter of the tree, a cold drizzle was falling. The park was closed for the night, but there were lamps on. The mix of orange illumination and the diamond sparkle of the speckled rain was somehow romantic and calming and cosy.

His empty stomach forgotten, Toby trotted happily towards the main gates, and the gap in the fence to the right of them.

"Good evening, lad."

He didn't see Rory appear or approach, but there he was, standing right in front of him. Toby stopped and regarded the old man warily.

"This is the second time we're seeing each other despite you saying we shouldn't see each other again," Toby said. "Third time, if you include ... the other night."

Rory nodded. "Let's walk."

It wasn't a request. Toby acquiesced but kept a slight distance between them. He didn't want Rory to reach out to grab him and spirit him away.

Not on an empty stomach!

"I felt I owed you one final visit," Rory said. "To thank you, more than anything. But also to make a confession." He cleared his throat. "I first met Minovska over a century ago."

Toby blinked at Rory.

"She'd arrived from Russia. A witch. We moved in the same circles. I was young. Foolish. We were ... involved. I didn't know how notorious she was overseas." His laugh was bitter. "I soon found out, though. Her practices, even then, were satanic. She was power-crazed. Ambitious. Insane. She would get what she wanted by any means. Usually through the foulest deeds."

"She struck me as that type," Toby agreed. *And really, really scary!*

Rory sighed. "We've been trying to locate Minovska for a long, long time. She vanished, and we were unable to track her down. We always had a feeling that the woman you know as Miranda Dervish, Minovska's daughter, would invite her back to Blackwell Manor at some stage. That proved to be the case."

They paused for a moment, staring out at the inky water of the lake. The drizzle, so light, barely disturbed the surface.

"Miranda's weakness was a desire to be at *home*. She was born here in East Devon, in Blackwell Manor, at the end of the First World War."

Toby opened his mouth to protest. That was impossible. Miranda Dervish could not be that old!

Rory held a palm out to Toby. "I know. I know. You'd never guess her age. This is where black magick leads. It's what Minovska is capable of. Miranda always wanted to live at Blackwell Manor but could never afford the restoration. By persuading her mother to return, she was able to attract wealthy and powerful donors to support her cause. They expected something in return, of course, but at least now they'll never get it."

"Will you go after them?" Toby asked, abruptly reminded of Ed taking photos of number plates outside the manor.

"No need. These people won't give *us* any problems." Rory snorted. "They're among the most corrupt members of mundane society, but I'm afraid that's for humankind to sort out. Not us."

"You told me you weren't a wizard anymore," Toby reminded him. "That wasn't the truth."

"I stretched the truth," Rory admitted. "I'm retired. But ... perhaps in my line of work, wizards can never genuinely retire. Not when there are monsters like Minovska walking free."

They resumed their stroll. "The fates brought us together, Toby. We should be grateful for that. Without your quest for vengeance, I might never have had enough information to pass on to the others. We were able to act because of you. I can only apologise that I didn't explain what we had planned sooner."

"You sent the wreath to Clarissa," Toby said.

"I did. I'm sorry. I didn't mean to upset her, but my order wanted to galvanise you both into taking action." Rory hung his head. "We were using you as bait. It worked, but it was ... unpleasant."

Harrumph, thought Toby. *Unpleasant? It was*

completely terrifying for poor Clarissa and Ed! They're suffering with PTPWD! Post-traumatic Pointy-Woman Disorder.

"I want you to know we are grateful. Extremely grateful." He stopped walking again and turned to face Toby. "I have left something for you at home. A token of goodwill. It's a grimoire I put together when I was a young apprentice. I hope it will help you become the wizard you want to be. The letterbox was superglued, so I took the liberty of unsticking it. I hope that's alright."

"Ah," said Toby. "Thank you. I forgot about that."

Rory sank into a crouch and wrapped his cool, arthritic fingers around Toby's head. "I have a message for you from Joseph ..."

Was it Toby's imagination, or was Rory's form becoming less solid?

"You have many gifts. Be aware and be wary," said Rory, his voice beginning to fade. "Remain curious and kind. Do good work. Be a true friend to all." Toby could barely feel Rory's hands at all now. "And know that I will love you for all of time."

The voice faded completely.

Rory had vanished.

Toby whined softly and blinked back sudden

tears, staring at the lights glinting on the lake, reflections of streetlights, perhaps, or something altogether more magickal. At home, Clarissa and Ed—who adored him and he them—were waiting for him, but for now, he relished the feeling of closeness he shared with his first love.

"I will, Old Joe," Toby promised. "I will."

COMING SOON

Fancy reading more of Toby's adventures?

Another One Bites the Crust: Spellbound Hound Magic and Mystery Book 8

Holy baguette!

A brand new bakery has opened in Sun Valley. Cue a frenzy of excitement among the locals as they snap up the much heralded baker's marshmallow muffins, terrific treacle tarts and berry spectacular Bakewells.

Toby, our beloved spellbound hound, is first in the queue to taste test the freshly prepared sammiches!

But when a spate of fatal poisonings shakes the local community to its core, it transpires Devon splits and Dorset knobs might be deadlier on the waistline than first thought.

There appears to be only one obvious suspect. However, in the interests of his favourite favourites, Toby wants to dig a little deeper. There's a rat in the kitchen ...

And it isn't Sal!

Available for preorder on Amazon.

ALSO BY JEANNIE WYCHERLEY

Spellbound Hound

(in reading order)

Ain't Nothing but a Pound Dog: Spellbound Hound Magic and Mystery Book 1

A Curse, a Coven and a Canine: Spellbound Hound Magic and Mystery Book 2

Bark Side of the Moon: Spellbound Hound Magic and Mystery Book 3

Master of Puppies: Spellbound Hound Magic and Mystery Book 4

Dem Bones, Dem Bones: Spellbound Hound Magic and Mystery Book 5

Born to be Styled: Spellbound Hound Magic and Mystery Book 6

Up, Pup and Away: Spellbound Hound Magic and Mystery Book 7

Another One Bites the Crust: Spellbound Hound Magic and Mystery Book 8 (Release Autumn 2024)

The Complete Wonky Inn Series

(in chronological reading order)

The Wonkiest Witch: Wonky Inn Book 1

The Ghosts of Wonky Inn: Wonky Inn Book 2

Weird Wedding at Wonky Inn: Wonky Inn Book 3

The Witch Who Killed Christmas: Wonky Inn Christmas Special

Fearful Fortunes and Terrible Tarot: Wonky Inn Book 4

The Mystery of the Marsh Malaise: Wonky Inn Book 5

The Mysterious Mr Wylie: Wonky Inn Book 6

The Great Witchy Cake Off: Wonky Inn Book 7

Vengeful Vampire at Wonky Inn: Wonky Inn Book 8

Witching in a Winter Wonkyland: A Wonky Inn Christmas Cozy Special

A Gaggle of Ghastly Grandmamas: Wonky Inn Book 9

Magic, Murder and a Movie Star: Wonky Inn Book 10

O' Witchy Town of Whittlecombe: A Wonky Inn Christmas Cozy Special

Judge, Jury and Jailhouse Rockcakes: Wonky Inn Book 11

A Midsummer Night's Wonky: Wonky Inn Book 12

Halloween Heebie-Geebies: Wonky Inn Book 13

Owl I want for Witchmas is Hoo: A Wonky Inn Christmas Cozy Mystery

Oh Mummy!: Wonky Inn Book 14

Pieces of Hate: Wonky Inn Book 15

The Faery of Witchmas Past: A Wonky Inn Christmas Cozy Special

Wonkytonk Witch: A Wonky Inn Mystery (Release 14th June 2024)

A Wonky Apprentice: Wonky Inn Book 17

A Barbarous Band of Blood Brothers: Wonky Inn Book 18 (Release May 2024)

The Witchy Wood and the Weirdly Wyse: Wonky Inn Book 19 (Release TBC 2024)

Wonderland Detective Agency

Dead as a Dodo: Wonderland Detective Agency Book 1

The Rabbit Hole Murders: Wonderland Detective Agency Book 2

Tweedledumb and Tweedledie: Wonderland Detective Agency Book 3

The Curious Incident at the Pig and Pepper: Wonderland Detective Agency Book 4

A Tragic Tea Party: Wonderland Detective Agency Book 5

The Pool of Tears: Wonderland Detective Agency Book 6

Into the Labyrinth: Wonderland Detective Agency Book 7
(Release TBC 2024)

The Municipality of Lost Souls

Midnight Garden: The Extra Ordinary World Novella Series Book 1

Beyond the Veil

Crone

A Concerto for the Dead and Dying

Deadly Encounters: A collection of short stories

Keepers of the Flame: A love story

With Peter Alderson Sharp

The Creature from the Grim Mire: A humorous Sci-fi, Time Travel and Alien Contact Mystery

---

Non-Fiction

Losing my best Friend

Thoughtful support for those affected by dog bereavement or pet loss

---

Follow Jeannie Wycherley

Buy me a coffee

www.buymeacoffee.com/jeanniewych

Find out more at on the website

www.jeanniewycherley.co.uk

Or visit her on Facebook for her fiction

www.facebook.com/jeanniewycherley

Follow Jeannie on Instagram (for bears and books)

www.instagram.com/jeanniewycherley

See Jeannie on Tiktok

@jeanniewycherley

Sign up for Jeannie's newsletter on her website

www.subscribepage.com/JeannieWycherleyWonky

Printed in Great Britain
by Amazon

60886568R00194